"Don't get o... ...,
Kody shouted. "It's a trap!"

Reagan screamed and pressed her fingers to her temples. By the time Kody reached her a second later, she was crying and holding her head in her hands. "Make them stop!"

He threw one quick look to the SUV—where a monofilament line that was almost invisible to the human eye ran to the underside.

"Hell," he muttered as he grabbed Reagan and took off running. Just as they reached his pickup, he heard an ominous click. With no time left, he dropped to the ground, taking Reagan with him. Rolling under the truck's cab, he covered her body with his own.

And the world exploded around them.

Dear Reader,

The Navajo call themselves The People. They call their philosophy "Walking in Beauty." We who respect this ancient wisdom can apply their unique philosophy of emotional balance and resilience to our own wellness and creativity—and improve our daily lives.

Though based on respect and grounded in reality, this book is a work of fiction. Some of the places, words and legends can be found if one takes the time to visit or study the Dine; others are strictly out of my imagination and aren't on any map or in any college class. For all who wish to add to their understanding of The People, here are a few simple terms. Some are traditional spoken usage and cannot be found in any dictionary, others are defined in *Diné Bizaad: Speak, Read, Write Navajo* by Irvy W. Goossen (The Salina Bookshelf, Flagstaff, Arizona, 1995):

Dine—The Navajo
Dinetah—The land between the four "sacred" mountains where legend says the Dine began and where many of them now live (the "four corners" Big Reservation that encompasses parts of Arizona, New Mexico, Colorado and Utah)
alni—A person who walks the line between traditionalist and modern cultures
anali—Grandmother (paternal)
atsili—Younger brother
azee'—Medicine
bilagáana—White (as in "white man")
chindi—The dark spirits who come with death
hastiin—Mister, the title for a respected clan elder
hataalii—Medicine man
hogan—The traditional housing of the Navajo, built in a round design and now mostly used for religious purposes
ya'at'eeh—Hello
Yei—The gods of Navajo myths. Holy people who emerged to the earth's surface through a reed

Best wishes,

Linda Conrad

LINDA CONRAD
SHADOW FORCE

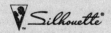

INTIMATE MOMENTS™

Published by Silhouette Books

America's Publisher of Contemporary Romance

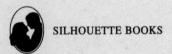 **SILHOUETTE BOOKS**

ISBN 0-373-27483-1

SHADOW FORCE

Copyright © 2006 by Linda Lucas Sankpill

Visit Silhouette Books at www.eHarlequin.com

Printed in U.S.A.

LINDA CONRAD

Award-winning author Linda Conrad was first inspired by her mother, who gave her a deep love of storytelling. "Actually, Mom told me I was the best liar she ever knew. And that's saying something for a woman with an Irish-storyteller's background," Linda says. In her past life Linda was a stockbroker and certified financial planner, but she has been writing contemporary romances for six years now. Linda's passions are her husband, her cat named Sam and finding time to read cozy mysteries and emotional love stories. She says, "Living with passion makes everything worthwhile." Visit Linda's Web site at www.LindaConrad.com or write to her at P.O. Box 9269, Tavernier, FL 33070.

To Natashya Wilson, for her dedicated work on my behalf and for giving me the faith to work on a unique and risky series like the Night Guardians. Thanks!

Chapter 1

Reagan Wilson took one quick last look at the crappy rental car, jumped in the shallow creek and ran for her life through the terrifying night.

This was one hell of a way to die.

She could just picture her obituary: "Noted mathematician dies in swarm of killer bees." Her cold, lifeless body would be found swollen up to twice its size. It could take days to identify her corpse.

What had she done to piss off bees this much? All she'd needed to do was get into the trunk and retrieve the spare tire and tools to change her flat. And hadn't she read in *Scientific American* that bees didn't swarm at night?

Now she would never have a chance to do anything, not research bee swarms or even lodge a complaint with the rental car company. She'd be dead, and those no-good jerks would simply rent that piece of junk to someone else.

The angry noise the bees made as they closed in around her bored into her brain like the nasty buzz of a dentist's drill. Batting them away and gulping for breath, Reagan cursed her shoes as she slipped on the sharp rocks of the creek bed. She loved these old Bruno Magli loafers, but they weren't worth a dime when it came to running for her life.

God, what was she thinking? She wasn't a trained marathon runner. She could never outrun bees. And her brand-new athletic shoes were packed away in her suitcase. The only sport she knew anything at all about was golf. And that probably wasn't going to do much to save her life.

Funny what went through a perfectly reasonable brain right at the moment of death.

Panic must be setting in and turning her scientific mind to mush. The mind that she'd inherited from her father.

Oh, Dad, are you out on this Indian reservation somewhere, battling for your life, too? Am I going to die never knowing what really happened to you?

Reagan brushed bees out of her eyes and stumbled up to her ankles in the frigid water. Water. If only it were deeper.

A blinding flash of light coming from her right made her trip over her own feet. Was it an hallucination?

"Drop into the water!" a deep male voice demanded.

Water? What water? The tiny trickle in this creek wouldn't even cover her big back end. Confusion caused her to miss a step, and she hesitated long enough to feel the nasty jolt of several stings.

Out of the black cloud of bees surrounding her, a huge fist grabbed her by the forearm and yanked her right off her feet. She was pulled—hard—and went down on her knees. The next thing she knew, something jostled her from behind and, just as the bees began to enter her nostrils and cut off her air, she was fully submerged in the iciest water imaginable.

The shock took her breath away.

Was she dead? For several seconds, Reagan couldn't feel a thing. Even her brain became numb from the cold.

She lost track of how long she was under the water, but knew humans could only hold their breath for a couple of minutes tops. When she lifted her head to take a gulp of air, a rough hand grabbed her by the back of the collar and dragged her to her feet.

"Can you stand?" The dark shadow of the man who had saved her life stood there, holding her shoulders with a firm grip.

Could she? Still waist deep in cold water, Reagan's whole body was beginning to quake as the gentle night breezes blasted through her soaked clothing.

Could she stand alone? Hell, could she breathe?

"I...I..." As cold as she felt, scientific theory would suggest that her body should be shrinking as her blood vessels constricted. But her tongue didn't feel smaller. No, her tongue felt swollen and unmanageable.

"Anaphylactic...shock...bees..." She was fast becoming light-headed as her airways swelled and closed.

"Hang on."

All of a sudden she felt as if she were flying. Her savior had picked her up and was splashing through the black night closing in around them.

Minutes passed. Or maybe hours. Her own raspy breathing grew fainter in her ears.

She was lying on solid ground. And from above, she heard vague mumbling through the fog in her brain. The notes coming from a deep male voice sounded just like singing.

A lullaby? Or a funeral dirge?

As the light-headed feeling began to shut down her brain, she gave up and let a new warmth surround her. If this was to be her end, it wasn't so bad.

At least, for the very first and last time in her life, there was someone there to hold her hand.

Kody Long cursed the cold as he forced his fingers to do what he wanted them to do. He had already scraped off all the stingers he could find, and he'd applied the whitewash paste to every inch of uncovered skin on the Anglo woman's hands, neck and face.

She wouldn't be pleased to know he'd stripped her down to check her entire body, but fortunately, the skin under her clothes had appeared unscathed. Thankfully, she'd worn long pants and a jacket against the late winter chill.

The black lace bra and panties had been a real surprise to him. It made him curious about her.

And, ah, how like the soft side of a rabbit's fur her skin had seemed when he'd touched her body. He had to admit it had been much more difficult to dress her again than it should've been for a man who prided himself on being a stoic.

There was nothing more he could do for her now but continue the chants that would complete the healing ceremony and ward off the evil venom. He had found her in time.

When he'd first picked up the familiar vibrations of preattack this evening, he had worried that somehow he'd missed warning a member of the Dine. Tonight's regular surveillance had been interrupted hours ago with the classic high-pitched whistles that usually signaled an imminent attack by the evil ones.

He'd notified everyone to stay inside with their families. The enemies' vibes came as a complete surprise. Just as it had been a surprise to arrive at the point of attack to find a stranger—an Anglo woman—was the target of tonight's assault.

Who was the *bilagáana* woman who dared to venture alone across a desolate section of the rez at this late hour? Why had the enemy chosen to go after her?

Kody reached down to run a finger across her soft, pale cheek. Warm. And so full of life.

Without knowing why, he quickly glanced at her left hand and checked out her ring finger. Bare. And just why would that be any of his concern?

Kody would have to watch his step around this one. But she *would* answer his questions before he escorted her out of Navajoland. No doubt about it.

Reagan opened her eyes to find herself looking into the deepest, warmest, dark brown eyes she'd ever seen. As she came to her senses, she noticed a warmth spreading through her entire body.

She almost purred.

Trying to sit up, she was blocked by a huge hulk of a man and realized the warmth was coming from him as he rubbed some kind of oil on her hands. The strong smell of eucalyptus filled her nostrils. There were other, sweeter scents as well, but she didn't recognize those.

She tried to focus on her savior's face, but though the moon and stars illuminated most of the area, the stranger stayed hidden in shadow. She got an impression of darkness. Thick ebony hair and brown eyes. Dark clothing.

"Uh…"

"Ah, you are back with us," he said with a grunt. "Good.

How are you feeling?" He dropped her hands and sat back on his heels.

"I'm…" She took a quick inventory. All her parts seemed to be in working order. But without his hands on hers, the cold seeped inside her skin and began to chill her bones. "…cold. But otherwise, I think I'm okay."

"Are you feeling well enough to get up?"

"I don't know. Should I try?" Now that was a weird thing to say. Why ask a complete stranger for permission to stand on her own two feet?

Without answering, the stranger stood and reached down to help her up. He waited until she made sure she was steady.

She checked out her clothes and discovered no broken bones. "Bummer. I ripped the knees of my pants. Must've happened when I went down on the rocks."

"Pants can be repaired. But you didn't break the skin on your knees." He looked down at her with a strange expression on his face. "Who are you? What's your name?"

"Reagan. Uh, Dr. Reagan Wilson."

"Dr.?"

"I have a Ph.D. in mathematical theory."

"Well, Dr. Reagan Wilson, you may have a bruise or two, but you will heal from this attack quite nicely."

Attack? Oh, yes, he must mean the bees.

That reminded her. "You pulled me down. Where did you come from? And how did that creek suddenly have enough water in it to cover me?"

Ignoring her questions, he took her arm and turned her around. "My truck is right over here. The heater should warm you up in no time."

Keeping a firm grip on her arm, he marched her toward the outline of an old pickup sitting by the side of the highway. "I heard your screams when the bees attacked. Luckily, you were running toward the beaver pond. I just helped you into deeper water. You weren't stung very many times, and I scraped away all the stingers. You'll be fine."

She did feel fine. Amazing. She didn't seem to have any ill effects from her run-in with killer bees, but she also didn't remember screaming. The bees would've been inside her mouth if she'd opened it that far.

"How did you avoid getting stung?" she asked.

"The bees knew better than to attack me. When you went under the water, they grew tired of the hunt and disappeared."

The bees knew better? What kind of man was this?

A shiver of unease ran through her. He walked her up to the truck and opened the passenger door for her. The interior light went on and she caught her first glimpse of her savior's face.

She already knew he was a big man. Broad in the shoulders and narrow in the waist, he was probably six-three or six-four. Though she usually felt tall standing next to men, she was amazed that he towered over her.

Now, in the light, she also realized that he was Native American. His hair was almost black, though it was cut shorter than most pictures she'd seen of Indian men in magazines and in the movies. His prominent nose fit his other strong and chiseled features.

Wearing a black T-shirt under a jean jacket and dark denim pants, he resembled a shadow. But she noticed the shadow had a cell phone, several suede bags and a huge sheathed knife dangling from his belt.

It made her more ill at ease than ever. Who was he?

He helped her up into the seat and then went around to

the driver's side. When he had the heater turned up at full blast, he put the truck in gear and started it.

"Where are we going? Who are you, and what about my car?"

He paused at the edge of the highway and turned to her. "My name is Kody Long and I'm an FBI special agent assigned to this area of the reservation. We're going to my brother's office. He's a local tribal cop.

"Your car will be safe until daylight," her rescuer continued. "Would you like to stop and lock it up?"

"Yes. And get my luggage, too, please."

He nodded and pulled out onto the highway.

An FBI agent? He worked for the government. She wasn't exactly crazy about the U.S. government at the moment. They had tried to hinder her search for her father at every turn. It made her wonder if this man would try to get in the way as well. Or if he'd been sent to follow her and report on what she was up to.

Whatever his real motives, she was suddenly no longer afraid. "Are you from this reservation originally?" she asked.

"Yes. I am a member of the Dine."

"Dine?"

"That's the name the Navajo use to refer to themselves. It means 'family' or 'clan.' This is our homeland."

"Oh." She should've thought to do some research before dashing madly out to a Navajo reservation. It really wasn't like her to be so rash.

The truck rounded a curve and her car appeared at the side of the road ahead. "That was quick. I thought we must've been farther away than this."

"The creek runs parallel to the highway through here. You couldn't see it past the cedars and piñons in that little gully."

He pulled up next to her rental car, with its trunk still

wide open. Leaving his pickup running, he pulled on the parking brake and stepped out.

Reagan scrambled out of the truck and started dragging luggage from the rental car's trunk. Kody went to the front driver's side and reached inside.

"What are you doing?"

"I'm removing your purse and the car keys. You said you wanted them, didn't you?"

Well, that was rather odd. She hadn't really said that, had she? It was almost as if he could read her mind.

Once everything of hers was out of the car and it was locked up tight, they drove off down the unlit, lonely highway. For the entire time, they didn't pass a single car going in either direction.

She rubbed her hands together in front of the heater's fan and felt the smooth glide of oil. She'd almost forgotten.

"What's this stuff you put on my hands?"

"The back of your hands took the brunt of the bee attack. You had maybe a dozen stingers embedded there. I simply treated your wounds."

"With herbal oil? Isn't that a little strange for an FBI agent?"

Kody shifted slightly in his seat. "I've been trained in the ancient medicines and therapies. Before…before I got a scholarship to college, I was apprenticed with a Dine medicine man."

A medicine man. So that's what she'd sensed back there when he was rubbing her hands. He had an awesome bedside manner.

"Well, thank you for being there. I thought I was going to die. It was certainly fortunate for me that you just happened to be in the right place at the right time."

"Fortunate?" He hesitated. "Yes, I suppose it was."

* * *

"I work in research for NASA's Jet Propulsion Lab in Pasadena, but I'm here on a personal errand. I've come looking for my father," she told the two men who were seated opposite her at an old metal desk. "I got a late start from Albuquerque and managed to get turned around in the dark."

Reagan wasn't sure how much to confide to the two Navajo brothers, one a uniformed tribal cop, looking very much like a typical gorgeous Native American movie star except for his startling blue eyes, and the other her dark, brooding FBI agent savior, with his short haircut, piercing brown eyes and gentle hands.

"Is your father missing? Do you have reason to think he's somewhere within the Navajo nation?" the cop, Officer Hunter Long, asked her.

Her body felt nearly thawed out, but she was growing tired, and every inch of her ached beyond belief. Not sure she was up to an interrogation or to dodging questions she might not want to answer, Reagan tried to evade the whole discussion until she was stronger.

"Sorry if I haven't been making a lot of sense, but I'm suddenly exhausted," she hedged. "Can one of you take me to a motel so I can check in? I promise I'll come back tomorrow so we can talk after I call the rental car agency."

"Have you reserved a room at a motel? There aren't many around, and most of them are booked due to an intertribal council going on this weekend."

"What?" Oh, God, she really had rushed off without her brain, hadn't she?

Reagan never did this kind of thing. Normally, she researched every move. Double checked every step. Not planning before jumping right in was the antithesis of scientific axiom. It embarrassed her to think she had been so unsystematic.

Kody felt a twinge in the vicinity of his heart when he saw the woman's shoulders slump and her chin drop. She looked so lost and alone.

He'd never been lost in his whole life. But alone…now *that* he could relate to.

"We really need to ask you a few more questions tonight," he told her in as soothing a voice as he could manage. "But I can see you're tired. Why don't you go into the washroom and freshen up…maybe splash a little water on your face?

"Meanwhile, Hunter can start a new pot of coffee and I'll check with the motels. Maybe I can dig up a place for you to stay tonight."

He watched as her chin came up and she gave him a weak smile. "I'd appreciate it, thanks," she told him. She stood, picked up her overnight bag and followed him to the washroom.

Dr. Reagan Wilson wasn't strictly beautiful, Kody mused. Not like his ex-wife had been. Her nose was too narrow and long and her chin too square.

But Reagan stirred his blood whenever he looked at her. And when he'd touched her, something electric had sparked inside him. Something he hadn't felt in many years.

She was fairly tall for a woman, probably five-nine. And with her slender body, small but perky breasts and full, rounded hips, she was the stuff of men's dreams.

It was the tangle of shoulder-length red hair that really captured his attention. His fingers itched to glide through the silky mass of curls. To bring them to his nose and inhale the musky fragrance that belonged to her.

He was daydreaming about diving into that rusty cloud as he came back to the office and his brother's question brought him up short. "So what really happened out there?" Hunter asked. "I felt the trouble, and Shirley Nez called several hours ago to make sure one of us was defending against the attack."

"I'll call Shirley and explain." Medicine woman Shirley Nez was his mentor and an advisor to all the Brotherhood. If it hadn't been for Shirley, the Dine would've been decimated by now.

"It was killer bees this time," he told Hunter with a grimace. "Not particularly inventive, but effective."

"But why the *bilagáana* woman? What possible threat could she be to the evil ones?" Even in private, it was against a Navajo's better judgment to utter the name of the evil that had been a dreaded reality throughout tribal history and that now threatened to destroy all who stood in the way.

Skinwalkers. Just the name brought terror to those who accepted the truth.

He shrugged a shoulder in answer to his brother's question. "We need more information." Trying to keep his voice neutral, he reminded Hunter of the information they did have. "We know something new and different is going down with the enemy. There've been too many attacks, and too many bad vibes sounding false alarms over the last few weeks.

"And we also know the feds are concerned about those rumors of Middle Easterners who've supposedly been seen on the rez," he continued. "My field office is keeping surveillance around possible entry spots. Homeland Security has said they want to place even more agents on tribal land. Just in case."

"Yeah, I know. Your day job, right?"

"You know my work as a special agent was the first thing that brought me home to the reservation last year." And his mother's family, the Begay clan, had been horrified that he would introduce such outside influences into their midst. "The FBI's interests have not yet interfered with Dine interests. But in my gut, I'm starting to think both jobs are about to become intertwined.

"My instincts are seldom wrong," Kody said as he felt a scowl crawl across his face. "Something beyond evil…something really nasty…is headed our way. And I have to wonder if this Anglo woman hasn't brought some of that trouble onto Dinetah with her."

Chapter 2

Reagan used one of the rough brown paper towels to dry her face and hands. Hands that had finally stopped shaking. Looking at her image in the tiny washroom mirror, she shook her head and groaned.

Her face was haggard, her eyes wild and sunken. And that red rat's nest where her hair should be would never comb out in a million years.

She didn't ordinarily care about her appearance. Not much need, since she worked at a computer sometimes twenty hours a day.

Just who was there to look good for? No friends, except for the guys she worked with and all her online buddies. Definitely no lovers. The couple of family members she had left, not including her father, were thousands of miles away in Boston. She couldn't even remember the last time that her home phone had rung.

Or come to think of it, yes, she did. Her great-aunt Claire had called two weeks ago and left a message on the machine, explaining that her mother had been sent back to rehab. But that wasn't anything new. Reagan could barely recall a time when her mother hadn't been in and out of treatment.

But tonight, when the absolute last thing she should be thinking about was the way she looked, Reagan wished she was beautiful.

Giving herself a mental reprimand, she tried to banish the picture forming in her head of her dark savior. Reagan had not been prepared for the forceful…awareness—she supposed that's what it was—that hit her hard in the gut when they'd stepped into the office and she'd gotten her first clear look at his face.

Over the years, in all those math courses and then in the various computer labs, she'd worked side by side with every sort of man. Most of them would qualify as geeks, she supposed, though some, like her one and only sexual experiment, George Bartholomew, had been attractive.

But none had caused the same kind of extreme physical reaction as she'd had tonight when Kody looked into her eyes with that all-knowing stare. It seemed he'd perfected a way of seeing right through a person's body and directly into the soul.

The chill she'd experienced with that gaze came packaged with a warm rush of blood to the base of her spine. Hot and cold.

Now she had to decide how much to tell him and his brother about her father's disappearance. She'd been intending to ask the local authorities for help in locating her father—or at least in finding out if he'd indeed come to the reservation, as his buddy had claimed.

But that was before the local authorities included a

bronzed god who brought a tingle to her every nerve ending with just one look. And who caused her mind to go blank with a simple touch.

Oh, get yourself together, you geek. She chided herself for losing track of her mission.

She barely knew her father. What he liked to do, what he enjoyed reading. They hadn't even seen each other for more than a half hour in the last…well, maybe not since her mother had divorced him almost twenty years ago.

But that wasn't for lack of trying on Reagan's part. And just when she thought they might have a chance to get together, just when they were living within a short flight from each other, the father she'd always loved from afar had disappeared.

Pitching the paper towel in the trash and straightening her shoulders, Reagan prepared to face the two Navajo lawmen. They had to be able to help her.

All she needed to do was forget that the tall, dark-eyed one not only gave her erotic goose bumps every time he looked her way, but had also saved her life.

"Your father is a navy scientist working on a project at White Sands," he repeated slowly. Kody was trying to judge Reagan's truthfulness by reading her body language as she answered his questions.

How much of what she'd told him was a lie? And what was she so obviously leaving out of her story?

His brother was the tracker in the family. A man who could read the signs. And Hunter was superior at reading people, too.

But Kody was the one who had been trained to read people's body language at Quantico. The Bureau needed their agents to learn the secret language of liars, and how words could be manipulated to cover the truth.

So Kody had the edge in ferreting out treachery and cunning—a very useful tool when it came to being part of the Brotherhood and uncovering Skinwalkers.

Reagan nodded, and looked directly up at him from where she was sitting in one of Hunter's wooden interrogation seats. The miserable chairs were once used in the principal's office at the local boarding school. Kody remembered them well.

"What kind of a project is that?" he asked, using his most charming and friendly tone of voice.

She shrugged. "I don't know. It's classified."

"Well, now…" he crooned. "You're in research, too. Don't you and your father ever trade interesting, uh, research stories?"

"I actually haven't seen my father in many years. But even if I had, we wouldn't have talked about classified projects."

He heard the wobble in her voice when she admitted to not having seen her father. Kody didn't know whether that was caused by something that hurt her emotionally, or a lie. In a way, he hoped it was the former.

"I'm sorry," he began softly. "Have you and your father been estranged?"

She shook her head, but her eyes darted from side to side. A lie? Or yet another uncomfortable truth?

"Is that coffee ready?" she asked.

"Hunter will be back here with it in a minute. In the meantime, can you tell me why you think your father is missing? If you two haven't seen each other in a while, maybe he's simply gone off on a trip without telling you."

"That's just it," she replied. "I was supposed to meet him in Albuquerque. Both of us are due a little time off and we were going to…spend some time getting to know each other again."

"He didn't show?"

"No. I was worried, so I went to his apartment in White Sands to see if he was sick or injured." Reagan took a deep breath. "One of his neighbors told me Dad had left a few days ago to…uh, take his vacation…on this reservation."

Well, something she'd just said was a lie. But Kody would have to figure out what later.

"Since you seem surprised by that," he began, "I assume you two hadn't talked about coming here."

Once again she shook her head. This time she was telling the truth.

Hunter came bustling back into his office, carrying three steaming mugs. "Finally managed to stop watching that ornery pot long enough to let it boil," he said with a chuckle.

Reagan gratefully took one of the mugs and lifted it to her lips.

"Careful, little lady," Hunter cautioned. "It's damn hot. I just burned my fingers."

Hunter surreptitiously gave Kody the sign that he was prepared to take her prints off the mug whenever she set it down. They would at least find out whether she was who her I.D. said she was.

Reagan blew across the top of her coffee. "Thanks. I'm getting so groggy I can hardly keep my eyes open."

Kody leaned his butt against the desktop. "Reagan was just telling me that one of her father's neighbors in White Sands told her that her dad was headed for Dinetah."

"Is that so?" Hunter turned to her with raised brows. "Where exactly on the rez was he planning on going?

There's twenty-seven thousand square miles of Navajo-land, and over a hundred thousand people. You'll need to narrow it down."

"I didn't realize the reservation was that big," Reagan told him after she swallowed a gulp of coffee.

There it was again. That look she got that said she was in over her head and totally lost. A tiny bud of protectiveness blossomed in Kody's gut and began growing toward his heart, threatening to undo all his hard-earned professional cool.

The three of them remained silent for a few moments as they sipped coffee. He could see the wheels turning in her head as she decided how much to tell them.

"Well, the neighbor did say something about Dad going to visit Canyon de Chelly. That's fairly near, isn't it?"

Hunter shot him a quick sideways glance, then evened out his features to talk to her. "If your father was headed for Canyon de Chelly, he'll be easy to find. Visitors are not allowed to roam around the monument without an authorized Navajo guide."

"Really? Why not?"

Kody wanted to be the one to give her the answer. "Reagan, the Dine consider themselves an extension of what you call Mother Earth. We are as one with the land and we treat all nature with great respect. Please don't take this too personally, but tourists...non-Native American tourists...don't always have the same respect.

"Canyon de Chelly is ancient ground," he continued. "There are places within its depths that are sacred to the Dine, where no outsider is ever allowed."

"Oh, I see." She looked so tired all of sudden that Kody's resolve to finish his interrogation tonight, before she got her strength back, began to weaken.

He set his mug down and went to her, then put a steadying hand on her shoulder. "Why don't we finish talking about this tomorrow? In the morning, Hunter can check with the few canyon guides that are working this time of year and see if any of them have seen your father."

"Did you find me a motel room?"

"No, sorry. They were all booked."

"What am I going to do? My rental car is still back beside the highway with a flat tire. I'm so tired I don't think I could drive very far, anyhow."

"There were no vacant motel rooms, but I did manage to find you a room for the night."

She brightened and raised her head to look at him. "Oh, good. Where?"

"Let's gather up your things. I'm taking you home."

Her eyes widened and she raised her shoulders. "To your place? I don't think that's such a…"

He felt his heart grow lighter as his lips turned up in the first smile he could remember in many years. "Not to my place, exactly. But it's the place where I feel the most comfortable, and you will, too."

He tried to rein in the smile, but couldn't manage it. "I'm taking you home to my mother's. She's expecting us."

Fear bubbled up inside Reagan as she sat in the pickup's passenger seat and watched the winding asphalt roll by. What had she gotten herself into?

Luckily, she also felt a good deal of anger mixed in with the fear. Parts of the mess she now found herself in had not been her own fault.

If her father's superior at White Sands had given her a few honest answers instead of hinting that her father had somehow defected—of all the ridiculous things—with classified information, she never would've taken off in such a rush.

And if the car agency hadn't rented her a lemon with a fussy engine and bald tires, she wouldn't have had a flat by the side of the road. And if…well, she guessed she couldn't be too mad at the bees. They were just doing what came naturally.

She stopped looking out at the blacktop road and the broken white dividing lines flashing down its middle, and turned to focus on her savior. It seemed he was taking up more than his fair share of the pickup's front seat. She'd tried ignoring him and the physical reaction she'd been having to his overpowering presence.

He was so different from anyone she had ever known.

Unfortunately, that sudden uncomfortable thought brought back the shiver of fear she'd been trying to overcome. And it also brought with it the odd jolt of physical awareness she'd thought she had conquered back in his brother's office.

In all her studies, she'd never read anything about fear being erotic. But then she wasn't entirely positive it was true fear she'd been feeling whenever he was close.

"Are you sure your mother is okay with you bringing a stranger to her home so late at night?" Reagan asked, breaking the long silence between them.

"My mother would never turn away anyone in need. Unlike some, it makes no difference to her who she takes in…or when. She welcomes all who need help."

"Unlike some? What do you mean?"

"There is prejudice in Navajoland, Reagan. Though such thought is not part of the ancient traditions, a few who supposedly follow Dine teachings are nevertheless way over the top in their criticism of outsiders."

"A few. But not you or your brother or your mother?"

"No."

"What about your father? How does he feel about out-siders…or for that matter, strangers coming over in the middle of the night?"

"My father has been dead for many years. But when he was alive, he never felt prejudice against anyone. It would've been hard for him, considering that he was an outsider himself."

"Oh." Reagan couldn't think of anything to say. She didn't want to know such intimate details of Kody's life. It seemed out of place somehow.

On the other hand, she was about to spend the night at his mother's house. She guessed that was a fairly intimate thing for a person to do. It had been years and years since she'd even been invited to have dinner at someone's home, so she wouldn't know for sure.

"Was your father an, uh…Anglo American?" She thought that was the term she'd heard him use to describe white Americans. And judging by his brother's brilliant blue eyes, she imagined that their "outsider" father must've had light coloring.

She watched Kody nod silently in the glow of the headlights.

As they drove on through the dark night, each of them stared quietly out the wide windshield. Both seemed determined to keep their thoughts and dreams locked deep inside their own hearts.

Kody glanced across the front seat to where Reagan had fallen asleep. It was good that she could sleep on the way home. She needed the rest.

Her run-in with the Skinwalkers tonight must've taken a lot out of her. He knew it had caught him off guard.

Why had the enemy attacked an outsider this time? Was it simply because she was an Anglo and a stranger?

That was doubtful. The evil ones had never before struck out unless it could benefit them financially or would somehow bring them more power. They didn't just pick on someone for the fun of the kill.

Reagan moaned slightly in her sleep and shifted in the seat. Thick strands of rusty-colored hair fell over her face and covered one eye.

A vivid image jumped into his mind unbidden. An image of his fingers pushing that hair out of her face and then lifting her chin to place a searing kiss across those full lips.

The urge to hear her moans, coming under the assault of his caresses, was immediate and overpowering.

Hot, savage sex.

That wasn't something he normally let himself dwell on. He had vowed, along with the rest of the Brotherhood, not to take a wife again—not to begin building a family of his own—until the threat from the enemy had passed.

And one-night stands had never struck him as a terribly satisfying way of scratching an itch.

He stretched and tried to drag his gaze and his thoughts away from the woman next to him. But the truck's front seat had grown smaller. And it was way too warm in the cab of this pickup.

No matter who she really was, or why the evil ones had attacked her, she was too close and too compelling for him to ignore.

Chapter 3

Soft, dappled sunlight fell across Reagan's face, bringing her out of a dreamless sleep. It took her a minute to remember where she was.

Sitting up in bed and giving a cursory glance around the flowery wallpapered room, she thought back to last night's terror and the warmth that had come after it. Kody had brought her to his mother's house late last night.

He'd introduced them, then he'd settled her into a guest room that had been his own boyhood room, redecorated. Within minutes, he'd said good-night and told her he would return in the morning.

Apparently, he didn't spend his nights in his mother's home. Too bad for him, really.

The house was cozy and warm. But it was Kody's mother who had most effectively captured Reagan's attention and made her feel welcome.

Audrey Long was a short, thin woman with silver-gray hair and a clear complexion. Kody had inherited her startling, deep brown eyes. But on her they appeared fragile instead of intense, and they matched her other softly angled features perfectly.

After taking a quick shower, Reagan had to decide what to wear. She hadn't packed any fancy things because the reason for this trip in the first place was to hang out with her father. He'd mentioned scouting out pottery shops and doing some hiking.

She seldom dressed in anything but jeans and sweatshirts anyway. But today she wished she'd brought something nicer to make a good impression on Mrs. Long.

To make up for having nothing else to wear except an old MIT rugby shirt and a pair of well-worn jeans, Reagan slid into another set of black silky high-cut panties and bra. Her one indulgence, wearing fancy underthings, made her feel good from the inside out.

And no one ever suspected the truth under the geeky math freak's clothes.

"Oh, there you are." Mrs. Long turned and smiled as Reagan entered the kitchen. "Come. Sit down and talk to me while I prepare your breakfast."

"Oh, please don't go to any trouble. I'll be fine with coffee until Kody comes to get me." Reagan pulled out a chair and sat down at the oversize, rough-sawn-wood table.

"Nonsense. No one leaves my house without a full stomach. It won't take a minute to fix eggs and fry bread." The woman's voice was soft and melodic, sort of like someone singing a lullaby. "You look very nice this morning, dear. Last night you were obviously exhausted, but now you look well rested and fresh."

How strange that Mrs. Long would say just the exact right thing to make her feel comfortable.

"Thanks." Reagan watched her as she worked at the counter and then at the stove.

Her kitchen was painted a soft, sunny yellow and there were ceramic pots, heavy cooking pans and knickknacks about. To Reagan the room felt homey and comfortable.

On the table, next to a bowl full of fresh lemons, was a huge vase containing dried sunflowers. Very nice.

"Does Kody live far away? Will he be here soon?"

Mrs. Long set a plate of scrambled eggs down in front of her. "When Kody returned to his homeland a few months ago, he built himself a hogan to match his brother's on the family property.

"Neither one of my sons has been able to stay in their father's house since he was…killed."

Mrs. Long looked suddenly embarrassed to have spoken so bluntly. She lowered her eyes and turned back to the stove. "Kody lives just minutes away and will be here shortly, I'm sure."

"A hogan?" Reagan asked after she swallowed her first bite of eggs. It was the one thing she'd picked up from Mrs. Long's words that seemed safe enough to discuss.

"It's the traditional ceremonial house for the Dine. Perhaps Kody will show you what one looks like later today." She brought two cups of hot, black coffee to the table and sat down next to Reagan.

"I'd love to see it, but I'm sure he'll be too busy," Reagan told her. "I was kind of hoping to find my father today, anyway. I'm a little worried about him."

Mrs. Long put a gentle hand on Reagan's arm. "Kody and Hunter will find him. Don't you worry."

But that was just what Reagan was worried about. She had to find him first.

* * *

"She is Dr. Reagan Wilson of Pasadena." Hunter's voice came in clearly over the cell phone. "And her father is Commander Robert Wilson, U.S. Navy, currently stationed at White Sands. Just like she said."

"I hear the 'but' loud and clear in your voice, bro." Kody stopped walking toward his mother's place and turned his face to the sun. "What else did you find out?"

"Several things. First, her father didn't go off on any vacation. I have an old army buddy who's stationed at White Sands. I gave him a call this morning."

Kody held his breath, waiting for the bad news.

"Seems that Commander Wilson has been working on a top-clearance project. Three days ago he vanished, along with some extremely valuable plans that belong to the U.S. government.

"The rumor mill has it that he's defected or is preparing to sell out to the highest bidder," Hunter continued. "My friend says the latest word is that he's been spotted in Argentina or maybe in Egypt. It seems pretty unlikely he would still be in the U.S., this close to the base."

"That doesn't sound good. Does Reagan know about the rumor?"

Hunter didn't hesitate. "Not within my friend's scope of information. He did just call back with an update from base security, however. Reagan was checked onto the White Sands base day before yesterday, and she spoke to her father's C.O. twice." He cleared his throat. "I'm guessing that means she knows something."

Damn. Kody knew she'd been lying. He wondered what else she hadn't said.

"Just in case she knows a whole lot more than she's told

us, have you asked around about Commander Wilson
hiring a Navajo guide to take him to Canyon de Chelly?"

"I've checked with most of the registered guides. No
one by that name has reserved either a guide or a room near
the canyons. There's still a few, uh, *unregistered* guides I
can check with. If I can find them."

"Right." Kody was well aware of what went on.

He knew there were renegade Navajos who would
take outsiders onto sacred lands—for enough money.
And with all the poverty still in Dinetah, money could
be a great motivator.

"Can we get a picture of Commander Wilson to show
around?" Hunter asked.

"I imagine the Bureau will be able to fax one. I'll
contact the field office in Albuquerque. We should have
something by later today."

Kody bid his brother goodbye, flipped his cell phone
closed and fastened it onto his belt. He continued down
the low hill toward his mother's house and the very interesting and secretive guest he'd left with her last night.

"Family is all-important to us, Reagan."

Kody heard his mother's words, spoken soft and low,
as he walked into her mudroom. He stood silently for a
moment before going through the door to the kitchen so
that his mother could complete her thought.

Whether they were telling myths, legends or lessons
in life, Navajos tried never to interrupt when their elders
were speaking.

"We have two families," his mother continued. "Our
immediate family and the extended family of the Dine.
The first woman, Changing Woman, gave us the first four
clans. Now there are many more.

"We identify how we are human by the clans of our ancestors," she explained. "I am of the Big Medicine People, born for the Rock Group Clan. All who hear this will know who I am. When we know our clan, we will never be alone. Our ancestors will always be near us."

Our ancestors may always be with us but that doesn't mean we never feel alone, Kody mused. Or maybe that was just his Anglo side speaking up. He decided that, finished or not, it was time to interrupt his mother.

"It's a good thing the ancestors don't carry a lot of baggage with them," he teased as he entered the kitchen and kissed his mother's cheek. "There are enough generations to cause an acute shortage of storage space—not to mention a shortage of bathrooms."

He turned to Reagan and found a wide grin on her face. The sight of that smile brightened up the entire room and made him forget for the moment how much he distrusted her—and remember how much he wanted her.

"Good morning," he said, and matched her smile. To his great disappointment, her smile disappeared.

"You look rested," he managed to comment, instead of begging for her to smile once again.

"I slept well." She had been drying dishes and quietly folded the towel to signal she was finished with the chore. "I also ate well. Your mother insisted on feeding me breakfast. She's a wonderful cook."

He put his arm around his mother's waist and drew her close. "Yes, she has many creative talents." He placed another soft kiss on the top of his mother's head. "Did you show her your artwork, Mom?"

"No. Perhaps another time."

Releasing her, he decided not to make an issue of the art. His mother hadn't had the heart to take up her painting again since his father's death. It seemed the whole family had lost heart at the same time.

"We need to talk, Reagan," he said as he turned to her. "I left the pickup at my place. It's not far. Walk with me?"

"What about my luggage?"

"We can stop back by here and pick it up on the way out. Okay?"

"All right. Just let me get my jacket." She turned to his mother. "Thank you so much for everything, Mrs. Long. I don't know when I've felt more at home."

His mother very nearly blushed. Reagan couldn't have said anything that would make a better impression on a woman who valued home and family as much as Audrey Long did.

When Reagan met him in the mudroom, he looked down at her feet and shook his head. "Nice shoes. New?"

"Well, yeah. They're athletic shoes. They'll be great for walking." She hesitated, then must have noticed his skeptical expression. "Won't they?"

"I don't suppose you brought any boots with you?"

"Boots? I don't own any. Why?"

He took her elbow and turned her toward the door. "Snakes."

Reagan fought her way through the low brush and rocks on the side of the hill. But since Kody still had hold of her elbow and was walking at a racer's pace, she didn't have much of a chance to watch out for snakes.

Dressed in jeans, with a brown suede jacket and a black cowboy hat, he looked as if he belonged on the back of a horse instead of walking up a hill. She glanced down at his feet and realized he hadn't worn regular boots, either, but heavy suede shoes that looked a little like high-topped moccasins.

"It smells good up here," she sputtered as she finally managed to tug her elbow from his grip.

"That's the scent of cedars and yellow pines."

She slowed her pace, forcing him to slow as well to stay beside her.

"It's nice. But…" Reagan frantically tried to keep the fear out of her voice. "What kind of snakes live here?"

"Rattlers, mostly."

"Those are poisonous." She picked up her pace a little. "How come you don't have on boots if that's what you need for protection?"

"There's an old Navajo legend that says our Dine ancestors once made a deal with the snake. We do not eat snake meat and they in turn do not strike at us."

"Hmm. Your people sure have lots of stories and legends." She blew out a breath and kept walking. "If I promise not to eat snake meat, can I get in on the deal?"

The chuckle erupted from low in his chest and hummed along her nerve endings. That same old awareness was back, reeling inside her with maximum force.

"You're scientifically minded," he began without directly answering her question. "What do you know about our animal neighbors and friends?"

"Me? Not much. Just enough to be dangerous, I suppose. I thought I knew something about bees, but that attack last night was a complete surprise."

"Yes, it was," he said with such a serious expression that she nearly laughed.

"I take that back," Reagan stated as she tried to keep a straight face. With his sense of humor, he was going to love one of her geek jokes. "I do know a lot about worms."

"Worms."

"Yes, you know, the—"

"Computer virus variety," he broke in, finishing the punch line for her. "Very funny." But his face remained sober, and his eyes didn't tease the way they had before.

"We need to talk about finding your father," Kody said while he kept walking. "Hunter and I have asked around and it doesn't seem likely that he ever came to Navajo territory. Maybe his neighbor was lying to you. Or maybe the Navy has a point and he doesn't want to be found."

The flash of anger came swiftly, almost cutting off her air. "You checked with the Navy? You sound just like his C.O. My father did *not* defect. He would never do that."

"And you're sure because…you know him so well?"

She felt her shoulders sag, and something in her gut twisted. "You know I don't. But I do know he's had an honorable career and loves his country. And it makes more sense that he would want to come here."

"Why?" Kody stopped walking and turned to face her. "Why are you so sure about that?"

Well, here it came. Reagan was going to need his help. Her father had to be in some kind of trouble or he would've met her as they'd planned. She had to tell Kody the truth in order to make him understand. To make him help.

"My father has always had just one all-consuming hobby in his life. It's one of the few things I can remember about him from when I was a kid." She hesitated only a moment. "He collects and studies ancient American Indian artifacts."

Kody narrowed his eyes and folded his arms over his chest. "Go on."

"My father's neighbor…friend, really…told me Dad ran into another collector a few weeks ago in one of those online chat rooms or blogs he frequents. This other guy apparently had just returned from a trip to Canyon de Chelly and was full of stories of a secret stash of artifacts he'd found buried in a cave there. He—"

"Wait," Kody interrupted. "You do know, as I'm sure your father knows, that it is illegal to remove any artifacts or relics from reservation land."

"Yes, I know."

"That's why you've been so hesitant to talk about this." Not a question. Reagan knew disgust well enough when she heard it.

"You're positive your father is too admirable to sell out his own country," Kody growled. "But you're not so sure he wouldn't mind ripping off mine. Is that it?"

"That's not fair. What if Dad was planning on returning things that had already been taken? Or maybe he wanted to be sure this other fellow had found the real thing, and then after verifying it, Dad would inform tribal authorities of the new find on their land?"

The look on Kody's face told her that he didn't believe either of those two scenarios. "Do you know the name of the other collector?"

"Dad's neighbor couldn't quite remember. He said it was something like 'Ahmed' or maybe 'Hammad.' Something…Middle Eastern anyhow. He was sure about that."

Suddenly, Kody's expression changed from skeptical to a blank slate. "Middle Eastern, huh?" He grabbed her elbow and took off up the hill once again. "Come on, let's go."

"Go where? Are you going to help me find my father?"

"I called the rental car company this morning and told them to come pick up your car for credit," he grumbled instead of answering. "Now you have two choices. You can do what I had originally planned for you, and leave. I'll have someone drive you to the Al-

buquerque airport. You can fly home and let the authorities find your father. Or…"

He stopped so suddenly Reagan almost ran up his back.

"You called the car rental company? But how was I
supposed to get around?"

He turned to scowl at her, face-to-face. "You weren't.
You were going home."

Of all the nerve. "Who died and made you my boss?
This is a free country and I can make my own plans."

"No, this is not a free country. You are standing on sov-
ereign Dine land. And you will leave when we say you
will leave."

Uh-oh. He had her there. She really didn't have any
legal right to stay here at all. Darn it.

"Your second choice is to stay and assist us while we
look for signs of your father." His eyes were darker than
she'd ever seen them. Dark and beyond dangerous, with
sparks flashing warning signs. "But if you do stay, you will
have to be accompanied by one of us at all times. The rule
will be that you are never to roam around alone on the reservation. No exceptions."

"Well…" The noise that interrupted her thoughts was
more like a vibration than a real audio tone. It was a sound
unlike anything she'd ever heard before.

Kody blinked once. "It's daylight, dammit." He'd
mumbled the words absently, but then he quickly grabbed
her by the arm and yelled, "Run, Reagan. Follow me."

Run? Where?

But her questions were moot. After dragging her up the
hill for a few yards, Kody swung back and circled her waist
with his arm without missing a step. Before she knew
what hit her, she was being swept along, her feet barely
touching the ground.

A second or two later they topped a rise and Reagan caught sight of his pickup parked in front of a big round log house. The noise grew ever louder.

Kody moved fast. It all seemed like a blur. Within a precious few moments, he opened the truck door, threw her flat on her back in the front seat and then landed on top of her as the door slammed shut behind them.

Immediately, the bright sunshiny day turned dark as night, and the roar of a strange clicking noise outside the truck increased, drowning out all possibility of speech.

Minutes passed as she gulped for air underneath him. She should have been scared. Instead, all she thought about was the body of the gorgeous Native American man, lying so tightly against hers on this cramped seat.

She could feel every one of his hard muscles and rough angles as they pressed her down. He seemed to be mumbling something in her ear, but she couldn't make out his words due to the high clicking noise of whatever was outside the truck.

As the whisper of Kody's breath fanned her face, Reagan's nipples hardened, her skin grew damp and her heart raced more furiously than it had during their run up the hill. They were so close their legs were intertwined. She tried to inch away from him, while the smell of their combined sweat tangled together in her nostrils and quickly heightened the rest of her senses.

His essence surrounded her. Captured her.

The noise outside began to subside, and she realized Kody was chanting what must be Navajo words. He wasn't trying to soothe or stir her. She could not have understood what he'd said.

"I can't breathe. You'll have to let me up now."

"Okay. Just a minute," he mumbled against the sensitive skin of her throat.

That was all she could stand. "Please. Now." She pushed hard against his chest.

He lifted himself up on his elbows, and his dazed gaze locked on to hers. "Have you made your choice yet? 'Cause if you haven't, I know what I want. I want you to stay."

"What?" She couldn't think and couldn't believe what she'd heard. At least, not while the lower half of his body still pushed her down into the seat.

She looked deep into his eyes and saw the same passion burning there that she was feeling. So much for choices.

Ah, hell.

Chapter 4

Partially hidden by boulders and an aspen grove, the evil ones crouched in dappled sunlight, watching the Navajo FBI man and the troublesome *bilagáana* woman as the two stood on flat ground and straightened their clothing. Because it was broad daylight, the Skinwalker witches were still in human form.

"Well, we found out a couple of things." The one who, during the dark hours, could change himself into a snake turned to talk to his superior. "First, we now know we can control the insects and make them do our bidding even in daylight. That will be quite useful."

The other man, the headman of the Skinwalkers, the one who had rediscovered the ancient secrets and had learned how to use shape-shifting for gaining power, scowled.

He made a noise that sounded like a growl, low and

dangerous in his throat. The Snake's human skin crawled at the sound.

"Control is never a surprise, Snake. And soon we will capture enough power to laugh in the face of tradition and be able to change *ourselves* over in broad daylight."

"Yes, yes," the Snake agreed. "But we also found out that the FBI Navajo, that Brotherhood bastard who tries to balance between two worlds, is definitely protecting the woman. It was no coincidence last night."

The Snake feared little on the reservation, but he was deathly afraid of the man squatting next to him. The man who was gossiped about in terrified whispers across the land. The Navajo Wolf.

Waving away the Snake's words, the Wolf scoffed. "Last night we only wanted to scare her off. Make her stop asking questions and leave Dinetah. She was not worth the time to kill."

"And that has changed today?"

The Wolf raised one side of his human lip in a sneer. "Didn't you see the attraction between the two? I could smell the animal musk from here. Sexual attraction is power. We can use it to our advantage."

"How?" The minute the word came from his mouth, the Snake knew he had made a mistake. He tried to back up a step, but his master wrapped a vicelike hand around his neck.

"Do you fully follow the ancient myths and legends, reptile? Do you submit to the Skinwalker Way of making money, the way as given to us by First Man and First Woman and by Diving Heron?"

Paralyzed with fear, the Snake could only grunt in response.

The Wolf sniffed, sensed the Snake's fear and drew in

the power-filled emotion to make it his own. "We need time to finalize our deal with those Middle Easterners. The ones who have come to Dinetah are none too bright, but they can be deadly all the same.

"So instead of a distraction for us, we will make that Anglo daughter a distraction for the Brotherhood. We will keep her and the FBI half-breed together, running in circles and interested only in each other."

He knew the Snake would never fully understand that power, and not simply money, meant control. And control was everything.

"Perhaps the daughter can also help us control her father," the Wolf continued. "After her usefulness as diversion for the Brotherhood is over, we will use her to force the father's full compliance. Love is just another means of control. And all emotion feeds our need."

The Snake drew in a shallow breath as the Wolf relaxed the hold on his throat. But the Wolf kept one big hand draped loosely around the back of the man's scaly human neck in an unspoken warning.

"Will we use mind control on the daughter?" The Snake spat out a hiss. "She is supposed to be very bright."

The Navajo Wolf leered at the smaller man with snake eyes. "No *bilagáana* woman is smart enough to beat our ancient black magic. Is that not right, Snake?" he demanded with a snap of his teeth.

"I've been practicing." The Snake's voice shook as he squirmed under the other man's light grip. "And I think mind control is much easier to accomplish than the old ways must've been. You know? Those traditional ways where you had to be right next to the victim."

The Navajo Wolf almost smiled. "By all means. Use your new powers. Find out how far away you can be and still control her mind. The more we use the power, the stronger we become."

He licked his lips and ran his thumbnail down the cracked skin on the back of the Snake's neck. "I believe it would benefit us more if we begin eliminating the Brotherhood now rather than waiting until later. I'm convinced the Navajo FBI man is a weak link. It's good that he will become our first target."

The Wolf didn't much care for having to depend on underlings, so he resolved to pay close attention to this project. Eventually, all of the subjects, both white and Navajo, would be dead. Perhaps even this idiot snake could disappear with the sands of time.

"What was *that* all about?" Reagan asked Kody as she looked over her shoulder. "What were those creepy things?"

Kody shrugged and walked around the truck's hood. "Crickets. Some call then katydids. I wasn't sure at first…"

"Sure about what? And what the heck were you mumbling about back there?" Reagan tried hard to hide her trembling hands, jamming them into her pockets.

The handsome lawman didn't say anything more until he'd walked all the way around the truck. "Looks like everything is in order. Get in and I'll try to explain."

"Sure, okay," Reagan said as she plastered a phony grin on her face. She needed to sit and get her thundering heart back under control.

But before she could put her foot on the truck's running board, Kody moved beside her and held the passenger door open so she could climb in. When he took her arm to assist, she could feel the tension curling inside him. It moved through his fingers and flowed right into her. His face was a mask of calm, but she sensed his internal fight to gather strength.

It made her even more nervous and shaky than she had been with the crickets. She couldn't seem to breathe. Her throat was closing and a tremor ran through her body. Her feet were glued to the ground.

While she systematically checked off her own odd reactions, Reagan began to wonder if she was in shock. "Crickets aren't poisonous or anything, are they? I mean they don't sting like the bees."

Kody shook his head, but seemed impatient to get going. In a surprise move, he circled her waist with his massive hands and lifted her into the truck's passenger seat.

Yikes! Now she really was shaking. All over. She felt a red flush, due not so much to embarrassment as from just being touched, move up her body to her cheeks.

He must've felt it, too, because he stopped and stared at her with a stunned look on his face. *His eyes.* Those dangerous chocolate eyes seemed to see right inside her, unlocking all the dusty closed doors she'd thought were shut for good.

It made her think back a few moments to when all his hard angles and steely muscles had been sprawled across her. Her pulse kicked up a notch or two with the memory. A sensual awareness pulsed in her veins, bringing smoldering fire to all her body parts. It stirred her blood, until her breasts became heavy and tender and she couldn't seem to sit still.

Was this also a symptom of delayed shock?

No sense kidding herself. Almost positive that what she was experiencing was a form of pure, unadulterated lust, Reagan wished she was more familiar with those feelings. But she'd read enough about the physical manifestations of sexual desire to believe that's what was happening to her.

She grabbed her jacket lapels and pulled them across her chest, trying to hide the evidence of how her body was noticing him. Her nipples had puckered into tight little buds under her cotton T-shirt.

Before she covered up, Kody apparently noticed, too. He flicked a glance to her chest, then back up to her face, finally focusing on her lips. What could he be thinking?

Climb in and drive away was the only coherent thought Kody could manage at the moment. They had to get moving, for more reasons than one. He needed to force himself to back off from her temptation and promise. No woman had made him this crazed with desire, not since the divorce.

And what about those crickets, swarming so late in the season? It was just too much of a coincidence, coming close on the heels of the bee attack. A black force must've stirred the insects from their normal places.

Kody wanted the space and the leisure to consider all the possibilities. But with Reagan so close, he was having a hard time concentrating.

Though he would enjoy exploring his fascinating attraction to her, now was not the time. And more, this could not be the woman who made him break his vows. He didn't know enough about her. Was she some kind of enemy spy?

As much as he might like to put miles of highway between them for the sake of his concentration, such an easy way out was not to be. He had to keep her close for the investigation.

Slamming Reagan's door, he walked around the truck and climbed behind the wheel.

It was important for the Brotherhood to learn why the Skinwalkers had taken such a big interest in a stranger. The good guys needed to gather all the information they could on the enemy's methods.

And he was the best choice within the Brotherhood organization to handle this investigation. The mention of Middle Easterners had made that clear. All of a sudden his FBI investigation had become intertwined with his Brotherhood obligations in a very real way.

Like it or not, he was stuck with Reagan for a while. He steeled his resolve, vowed to reacquaint himself with the stoicism he'd apparently misplaced, and gingerly drove his truck down the gravel driveway. Without another glance in Reagan's direction, he sped right past his mother's house.

"Aren't we going to pick up my bags?" Reagan asked.

"Not yet. Maybe later."

He noticed the way the early morning sunshine gleamed on her hair. The rose and yellow rays gave those auburn curls a mellow, glowing effect. And now that he was noticing things, he could see her chin was strong but also feminine and fine at the same time. Her full lips, though naked of any makeup, seemed satiny soft and eminently kissable.

He chastised himself for once again giving in to the tantalizing distraction, and turned back to watch the road.

"You didn't answer me before," he began, still facing forward. "But you *have* decided to stay in Navajoland until your father's disappearance is resolved, right?"

"I guess if you're willing to help me search, I'd be foolish not to take you up on it."

Kody sensed her hesitation and discomfort as she squirmed slightly in her seat. "I can't promise anything,

Reagan. If your father is involved in any kind of artifact theft, he will be treated like all criminals."

"But—"

"*But* I'm willing to give him every opportunity to prove his innocence before we jump to conclusions. I've thought it over and it seems to me quite a coincidence that a man with no previous record is suddenly under suspicion of being both a traitor and a thief."

Actually, there were a couple other strange coincidences that Kody didn't trust, either. He intended to follow up on all of them before he allowed Reagan to leave.

"Oh. Okay," she said. Folding her hands in her lap, she stared out the side window as the green pines and blue spruce began to give way to ruddy-colored sandstone spires dotted with gray sage.

"It's pretty here," she said, sounding amazed. "Not at all like the desert I drove through in New Mexico."

"Dinetah landscape is as varied as its people. But I personally love the mountains and the steep cliffs. As we travel, look around and appreciate the beauty you see." He smiled to himself and decided to give her a lesson. "The People walk in beauty. It's part of our tradition, keeping everything in balance. Our art, our architecture. The land around us. Sometimes, we pay too much attention to beauty and forget that there are ugly things in the world."

As the words left his mouth, Kody was reminded of how out of balance his mother had been lately. She had turned her back on her art in a most non-traditional way.

In fact, the whole of Dinetah seemed to be moving out of balance since the Skinwalker raids had begun. Rubbing his hand across his jaw, Kody wondered if he was moving too far afield with Reagan. Balance and moderation had not lately been his strong suit, as much as he had tried to keep the lessons in mind. He dropped the Navajo Way discussion and vowed to stick to his investigation.

Lost in thought and staying quiet for too long, Kody should've expected Reagan to break the mood.

And she did. "Where are we going?"

"I want to question a few people who do business near the canyon's visitors' center. See if anybody there knows of your father." Kody resisted the urge to turn and look at her. "In particular, one of the reservation's original trading posts. In Three Eagles."

His head tilted toward her, despite his best efforts to avoid looking in her direction. "You wouldn't need a good pair of moccasin boots, would you?"

"Well, maybe." Reagan shifted in her seat. "Oh. I get it," she said after a moment's silence. "We need an excuse to stick around and chat with the locals at this store. I'm not much of a shopper...at least not in person. I get most of my clothes off the Internet. But trying on boots might be fun. And if they will help ward off the snakes, I'm all for it."

Kody couldn't stop a smile. "Tell me what your life is like back home, Reagan. I'm guessing you don't spend a lot of time outdoors."

It wouldn't hurt for him to understand more about where her heart and soul lay. She was right in the center of a growing investigation and had been a Skinwalker target at least twice. The more he learned about her, the better his chances were of figuring out why.

Reagan squirmed again, trying to move as far away from the heat of Kody's body as possible. This truck ride had seemed interminable so far. Another few minutes of breathing in the musky scent of the big man sitting in the driver's seat and the windows would be fogging up.

Maybe if she talked more, she could forget about being

stuck in this tiny truck cab with a man whose presence seemed to grow larger every minute.

"Are you too warm?" he asked as he twisted the heater control dial.

"A little." He was feeling the heat, too, she thought with amazement. "I've always liked the cold better. I'm an air-conditioning freak. I'm known at work as the sneak who's forever cranking it down to sixty-five."

She lowered her window a few inches and took a deep breath. "You're right about me spending most of my time indoors. There's a bunch of us at my lab who prefer odd hours. Sometimes we'll get into something interesting and just keep working around the clock. But I find I think clearer from dusk to dawn."

"When do you sleep?"

"I don't seem to need much sleep," she said with a shrug. "Three or four hours a night is about my limit. I'll usually try for a nap in the middle of the day."

Not wanting to mention how strange it seemed, she did wonder why last night at his mother's house she had fallen asleep a little after ten and slept clear through until six. It was the first uninterrupted eight hours' sleep Reagan could ever remember having.

"So you don't like any outdoor activities at all?"

"When I was in college I learned how to swing a golf club…just to please my mother's uncle, who believed in using a country club for business purposes. Amazingly enough, every once in a while some of the big shot dudes at NASA will organize golf days with the staff. My boss once actually told me that golf could clear your head. Open your mind to bigger possibilities.

"He didn't know how I play the game," she added with what she hoped was a sly smile.

Reagan saw the corners of Kody's mouth twitch. "And what's different about the way you play?"

She ran her fingers through her hair, trying to push the curls into submission and keep them off her face. "I deduct points from my score for not breaking into a sweat and for getting through the course with as little effort as possible."

"I see," Kody said in a neutral tone. "And how do you do that?"

"It's all in the math. Nearly everything can be done easier and quicker using mathematical formulas."

When he'd first found out where she worked, he'd wondered if she was a math genius. Looked like she probably was, but he didn't know yet whether that idea intimidated him or not.

"Ever apply those formulas to moneymaking propositions?"

"What? You mean like gambling?" She shook her head and rusty curls went flying. "Nope. I know people who do, but it's not my thing."

But she'd known immediately what he was talking about. "Then what is your *thing*, Reagan?"

"I'm not sure I actually have anything but work. Not in the way you mean, anyhow." She dug in her jacket pocket and came up with what looked like a handheld PC.

She held it out to show him, but Kody only gave it a cursory glance. "Tech stuff. Games. Music. Movies. Blogs. That's what I do in my spare time," she said.

"Sounds like a rather solitary life." And exactly what he had most dreaded in his own world. "Don't you ever get out with people?"

"Not so much. Just sometimes with the guys at work."

"What about your family?" He hesitated. "Except I guess for your father. You've already said you two weren't close but you were trying to change that. What about the rest of your relatives?"

He noticed it was Reagan's turn to hesitate. "My mother is alive. Back in Boston. Then there's her aunt and uncle. I talk to them on the phone every now and then. But none of us are close. I haven't seen them in several years."

"It sounds lonely." He could not imagine anyone wanting to cut himself off from human contact. In Navajo tradition, acting like you had no family or friends was the worst possible thing to do. Some even thought it bordered on criminal.

"Yeah, well, we geeks prefer it that way."

"You don't look like a geek." He meant that sincerely, but the words surprised him when they popped out of his mouth. "In my opinion, you walk in beauty."

And if he could get as close to her as his body wanted, he would prove his point. Every part of her was obviously in balance.

But he wasn't going to do anything even remotely like that. Not when it might botch up the investigation.

Reagan smiled. "Thanks. But it's the glasses. I gave them up for laser surgery a couple of years ago.

"I'm still a geek at heart," she added. "Just ask anybody who knows me."

Kody decided not to argue about it. He was right on the verge of saying what he really thought about her. And that would not be smart.

She folded her arms over her chest and stared out the window again. "You never got around to telling me about the singing. You were doing it when the crickets sur-rounded us, and I think I remember you doing something similar last night with the bees. What is that all about?"

The Three Eagles Trading Post came into view as the

truck rounded the last bend in the road. "I'll tell you about it another time. We've got shopping to do."

That is, maybe he would tell her. If he decided that she could be trusted.

Chapter 5

The Wolf stood alone, inspecting his reflection in the bathroom mirror. *He'd done it.*

Using the powerful sexual tension he'd stolen from the air surrounding the white woman and her FBI half-breed, he'd found the secret. He had actually accomplished the feat he'd been dreaming of for years. He'd become the Navajo Wolf—in broad daylight.

The system might need a little tweaking, and he needed to gather a bit more power in order to make it easier, but he now knew the answers.

Smiling to himself in the mirror as he straightened the knot in his tie, the Wolf, once again in human form, laughed as he slipped into his Armani suit jacket. The discovery had been such a triumph that he barely cared whether the Snake could handle the Navajo FBI man, or for that matter, bring in the commander's daughter.

He had been practicing his own method of mind control. And though he hadn't been able to get Commander Wilson to agree to defect yet, he'd managed to make headway with controlling the mind of the oil baron, Sheik Bashshar. Ha! What a joke these supposed terrorists had become. They had no idea of what *real* terror looked like.

Shrugging, the Wolf figured if all else failed, he would simply control the sheik's mind long enough to get him to wire funds into the Skinwalkers' offshore bank account.

The Skinwalkers might not even need the smart *bila-gáana* daughter—or her difficult father. The two could just as easily become a couple of dead Anglos. A statistic. Nothing more.

Like a lot of things on the reservation, the Three Eagles Trading Post was an uncomfortable mixture of old and new. Gasoline pumps had been put in a few years back, but the store still carried canned goods and clothes that looked as if they'd been sitting on the shelves for fifty years. Baskets, woven rugs and silver jewelry sat disjoint-edly alongside posters selling tickets for four-wheel drive Jeep tours and promoting throwaway cell phones.

The trading post itself had been built by a English trader in the late eighteen hundreds and soon became a local center of commerce. Today, one of that man's mixed Navajo descendants owned and ran the place.

His name was Bahe Douglas, and Kody had always gotten along with the guy. He'd felt they had an invisible tie. Both of them stood with one foot rooted in tradition and one foot running toward the white man's version of the future. The People had a word for it: *alni.* One who walks the line between two cultures.

"This place is fascinating," Reagan whispered as they walked through the open doorway.

Kody grasped her hand to keep her close until he could take stock of the customers in the store. And immediately wished he hadn't. At first contact, a jolt ran through his palm, leaped along the skin on his arm and skidded to a landing at the base of his spine. Whoa.

He heard Reagan gasp, so he lifted his gaze from their joined hands to her face. Catching her stunned expression, he guessed she'd felt the jolt, too.

She broke the contact before he could, and stepped back. "What do you want me to do first?" she asked with a rasp.

His mind filled with all kinds of inappropriate responses to her question. But he leaned closer without touching and whispered in her ear, "Just stay near and follow my lead. I want to check things out for a few minutes."

Reagan nodded, but she took two more steps away from him just the same.

Kody turned his attention in another direction. He had obligations, dreams and needs, and he tried to tell himself that none of them included her.

But apparently his body refused to accept the truth of their situation. Electric shocks of desire continued to echo through his extremities while he surreptitiously studied the rest of the people in the store.

And when he saw the proprietor coming in their direction, Kody discovered suddenly that he had to wage a pitched battle within himself. A fight that would enable him to find enough balance to actually open his mouth and utter a sound.

"Ya'at'eeh," the Navajo behind the twenty-foot-long

counter said as he came closer to where Kody and Reagan were standing.

"Ya'at'eeh," Kody replied politely.

He had known the proprietor of Three Eagles Trading Post for the better part of his life. He thought back to their school days and remembered that Douglas had been only eight years his senior. Today, though, the man appeared to have aged twenty years since the last time Kody had been in the store.

FBI training and traditional Navajo conditioning put Kody's senses on alert. He shook off the lingering effects of Reagan's touch and studied the older man as he took his outstretched hand in a Dine handshake that was a softer version of the white man's.

Douglas was a barrel-chested man with a round face and heavy bone structure. Typical of the Navajo-Pueblo Indian mixture prevalent on the reservation, Douglas was a half foot shorter than Kody, with a square jaw and thick eyebrows. He wore jeans and a plaid western shirt, with more jewelry than most modern men on the reservation would consider tasteful—a silver squash-blossom necklace, four or five silver-and-turquoise bracelets running up each arm and a silver concho belt buckle that must weigh half a pound. Everything was far too flashy.

Hatless at the moment, the proprietor's long hair seemed to have become more gray than black in the few weeks since Kody had last seen him. Douglas wore it pulled back in a braid.

Kody didn't want to stare, as that would be an extremely rude thing for any Navajo to do. But when he shook Douglas's hand, he couldn't help but notice his face had changed. Lines had appeared at the corners of his eyes and mouth that had not been visible a few months ago.

Either the trading post owner had spent far too much time in the sun without a hat, or some kind of unusual stress had taken a terrible toll on him. Navajo skin did not sunburn, but could become dry and cracked with enough harsh sun or due to advanced age. This time of winter, Kody felt sure the sun could not be to blame.

Douglas's looks made Kody wonder if maybe the Skin-walkers had been stalking the locals on this part of the rez and he just hadn't heard about it yet. He would have to tread with care when he questioned Douglas. If his old friend's aged appearance was due to fear, it would be particularly difficult to get any information from him.

The Skinwalkers knew all about trafficking in fear and terror. They were masters at it.

Reagan hung back and let Kody's broad chest partially shield her from view while he spoke softly in Navajo to the man behind the counter. Taking in as much of the interior of the trading post as possible from where she stood, she waited while her shaky body used the time to simmer down.

The place was crammed with artsy things on every surface. The corners were dark and shadowy, but she could see paintings, baskets and leather jackets painted with Indian designs hanging on the walls. Along the main aisle were row after row of glass jewelry cases that made her think of other gift stores she'd visited. She would've liked to get a better look, but didn't want to move until Kody said it was okay.

Reagan wasn't normally so cautious, but that last touch of his hand had been mind-bending. It had done things inside her that moved well beyond her experience. Something foreign had rolled right through her veins, making her hypersensitive and muddled. A strong rush of adrenaline would've done the same kind of thing, but there had been nothing to cause such a reaction.

Confusion was not one of Reagan's normal states. But when she'd calmed down enough to have a clear thought, it occurred to her that maybe her hormones had somehow spun out of control. Had she eaten something funny to cause that?

Shifting from one foot to the other, she glanced around at the other customers in the store and was glad they hadn't appeared to notice anything odd about her behavior.

When she and Kody had first come inside, six sets of eyes had turned to see who had entered the trading post. Now the five other customers were quiet and probably listening to the conversation between Kody and the man behind the counter. None of them were looking in her direction.

That gave her an opportunity to check them out a little more. The young couple standing near the cash register seemed like tourists. A bleached blonde, the girl wore a halter top and sunglasses despite the fifty-degree temperatures outside. Her husband, or perhaps her boyfriend, wore denim, like every man in the store. But he also had a neatly trimmed beard and bushy hair. He looked more Italian or Latin American than Native American.

She shifted her gaze to the two Native American women who were rummaging through a pile of pants on a sale table. One wore a colorful, old-fashioned skirt that came down to her ankles and a bright blue ski jacket made out of waterproof and breathable materials. Reagan recognized the jacket from one of the online auction sites she frequented. It was brand-new and expensive.

The other woman with her looked to be about fifty and

wore frayed denim. She had a fleece cap pulled down over her head, covering her ears, with long, dark, tangled hair falling from underneath.

One more customer stood off in a corner, looking at paintings. He was standing in a partial shadow with his back turned to her. But Reagan could see that he was several inches taller than her five-nine, and he looked even taller due to the black felt hat he wore.

One fat braid hung down under the hat and flopped against a brown leather motorcycle jacket. The customer seemed lithe and wiry under the coat. Even from a distance, there was something about him that made her uneasy.

"Reagan Wilson," Kody said, recapturing her attention. He gestured toward the man behind the counter. "This is an old friend. The post's owner, Bahe Douglas."

She shook the man's hand over the wide counter.

"He runs the place," Kody continued. "But he's short staffed at the moment."

"You go right on over and look at the boot display, young lady," Mr. Douglas told her. "I'll be there to pull your size as soon as I help these other customers."

"Okay. Thanks."

Kody led the way through the stacks of merchandise. "Take your time looking through the different styles," he whispered when they were out of the earshot of the others. "If anyone but Douglas comes over, you can start a casual conversation. But be careful what you say. I don't think you should mention your father."

"What's the matter? Why not?"

When he shook his head, the movement was almost imperceptible. "Something feels wrong."

Reagan's heart jumped into her throat. "What?"

"Just keep cool and study the boots. Douglas will be over to help you when he's free. In the meantime, I'll try catching the latest gossip from the old women, and see if I can pinpoint where these unusual vibes are coming from."

"Unusual vibes?" she croaked in the loudest stage whisper imaginable. And earned herself a glare from Kody as a response. He turned and made a point of casually strolling away. What on earth had he meant by *unusual vibes?* Were there some kind of *usual* vibes? Reagan had been getting all kinds of strange sensations.

Or…maybe that wasn't exactly true. Every time Kody came within two feet of where she stood, her body started to hum. Was that what he'd felt, too?

By the time she turned around to look at the selection of ladies' boots, Reagan was shaking her head. It was bad enough that she was a total nerd when it came to relationships with real live people. Her element was the Internet. That's where she was comfortable.

So what was she doing here on the Navajo reservation, seeking information from strangers that made her too nervous to think? And worse, why was she taking orders from a virile, handsome FBI agent who gave her the shakes whenever he came close?

Talk about being out of your element. She couldn't think of one single thing that had happened to her in the last twenty-four hours that could be classified as *normal.*

Unusual, he'd said. Ha! Try freaking weird, crazy, mixed up and totally from another planet.

Reagan took a deep breath and reminded herself that she'd come to find her father. The longer she went without hearing anything from him, the more she was convinced that something terrible had happened.

So whatever she did or didn't feel shouldn't matter. She would stay. Stay on the reservation, and stay glued to Kody until they found her dad.

"Those boots without a heel would be best for walking in this part of the country."

Reagan jumped when a deep male voice came from beside her. She turned to find that the strange guy with the leather jacket and long braid was standing a few feet away and seemed to be studying her instead of the shoes. How did he get that close without her hearing him?

She nearly bit her tongue to keep from screaming. "These?" she asked in a shaky voice as she pointed to a pair of dark brown, midcalf suede boots.

He nodded, but his fierce gaze never wavered from her face. The rim of his hat threw a shadow across his eyes, but Reagan got a good look at them anyway. They were so flat and black it made her wonder if the pupils were dilated.

"Ya'at'eeh." Kody's voice came from behind her.

Sneaking a peek in the FBI agent's direction, she discovered his attention was focused not on her but on the stranger. Reagan decided to keep her eyes on the boots and to stay quiet.

"Ya'at'eeh," the stranger replied casually.

Kody asked the man something in Navajo that Reagan didn't understand. The man answered in the same way and she felt a chill crawl up her spine at the sound of his voice.

She'd already noticed that Navajo was a guttural, earthy language, mostly spoken in soft tones. But the sound of the odd guy's voice was just plain creepy.

As Kody spoke to him, he straightened and his eyes narrowed. Despite the soft tones, something confrontational was going on between the two men.

Kody suddenly put a hand on her shoulder. "This

woman has come seeking her relative," he told the stranger in English. "The Law and Order have agreed to help her search. The man she looks for is Anglo and is known by the name of Robert Wilson. Have you heard of such a man?"

Reagan was having a hard time thinking with Kody's hand on her body. There were so many things she didn't know about the FBI agent who had agreed to help her. But one thing was for sure. His touch was magic.

And it turned her brain to butter.

"Why would the law ask me?" the other man said in English. "I don't know him."

"Bahe Douglas tells me you sometimes give canyon tours for the tourists. The man we seek would have been interested in such a tour."

The stranger folded his arms across his chest. "The trading post man has his facts wrong. I have no tribal license for tours."

Reagan felt Kody's grip tighten on her shoulder.

"Perhaps you must travel in that country for other reasons. If you see such a man, you could tell him to contact his relative or the tribal police."

The stranger looked thoughtful. "What did you say he looked like?"

Kody turned his head to Reagan and asked, "Can you describe him?"

"Uh…" It had been so long, Reagan wasn't sure if she could remember what her father looked like. "Well, he's about five foot nine, with thinning, dark red hair and brown eyes. But there's nothing particularly outstanding about his appearance."

Kody faced the stranger again. "He is a white man, about the same height as this woman, and he might be found in areas that are not allowed for Anglos. It would be helpful for you to ask any white man you see over that way to give the law a call."

"There are rumors of witches on the slopes," the Navajo said with a grin. "It's only old-woman talk, but the People will not approach strangers in that area of Dinetah."

Reagan caught Kody's quick glance in her direction before his attention returned to the other man. "You don't believe in superstitious gossip."

The man still looked amused but he remained silent.

"We ask that you notify the law if you see a white man who is not in the right place."

Listening carefully, Reagan got the subtle change in Kody's voice and in his message. She kept quiet.

"It would be better if this woman's relative contacted her on his own," the stranger announced.

Kody nodded but said nothing more.

The strange Navajo threw a last furtive glance in Reagan's direction, then silently walked away.

Reagan released the breath she hadn't known she was holding. "Oh my God," she gasped. "That really creeped me out. He's not going to help us, is he?"

"We will discuss it later," Kody told her in a whisper.

"Yeah, but what was that about the witch—"

"Later."

"Yeah, okay. But…"

At that moment, Mr. Douglas came up the aisle toward them. "Are you ready now to try on a pair of boots?"

Rubbing the sleeves of her jacket, she tried to bring warmth to her chilled arms. Then she swallowed hard, but still couldn't get a word out.

"Take your time," Kody said to fill the silence. "I have a little more shopping to do."

He was going to walk away? Well, she supposed that was a sort of compliment. Kody must think she could handle things by herself.

She cleared her throat. "I'll be fine." To cover her nervousness, she turned back to Mr. Douglas. "I might want to buy a few pairs. What kind of plastic do you take?"

"Plastic? That is not one of the normal pawns we take in trade. Can you explain?"

Uh-oh. She was going to have to watch what she said. These people were apparently living in a time warp.

About half an hour later, Reagan finished paying for two pairs of boots, put her credit card away and then looked around to find Kody. But she couldn't see him.

She strode down the two long side aisles, but there weren't any other customers in the store. Returning to the cash register, Reagan was dismayed to find that even the owner was suddenly nowhere to be found. The hair on the back of her neck stood straight up.

Not normally a big fan of fresh air, she reached the open front door in two giant strides and took a big gulp of the stuff. Reagan could see that Kody's truck had been moved. She supposed he'd parked it next to the gas pumps for a fill-up, but she still couldn't see if he was with the truck or not.

On the far side of the pumps, an old van was parked, and another man Reagan didn't recognize was filling his gas tank. It only took her two seconds to decide that she should stay with Kody's truck. No matter where he'd gone, he couldn't go far without his transportation.

Reagan made it across the parking lot in record time, but when she realized she would have to inch past the stranger filling his tank in order to climb into the passenger seat, her feet slowed to a crawl. She came to a dead stop right behind the truck.

Looking around, Reagan had never felt so alone. It was just her and this other stranger, all by themselves in the wide open spaces. The highway was free of any traffic. The parking lot was suddenly empty. No one else was in sight.

She glanced up at a pine-covered ridge that towered above the trading post and wished she could enjoy the view, but she was too damn scared to do much of anything except breathe in the cedar-filled air.

"Smoke?" the stranger said all of sudden.

A gasp escaped her mouth as she stared at him.

"I frightened you?" he asked in a heavy accent.

The man was a short, wiry guy who didn't look Native American. Reagan thought he must be Mexican. His face was full of pockmarks and creases, so he might have been younger than he appeared. His jeans were filthy and full of holes and his long-sleeved shirt was the color of red mud. Holding one thumb on the gas pump, he offered her a cigarette out of his crumbled pack with the other hand.

"No," she said, meaning no to both. But he looked confused, so she clarified. "Thank you, but I don't smoke."

He shrugged, put the pack to his lips and withdrew a cigarette. After he crammed the pack into his pants pocket, he took out a cheap, throwaway lighter and lit up.

Reagan didn't know whether to lecture him for smoking next to the flammable gas tanks or to run like hell.

But without Kody, she wouldn't know where to go. She stood transfixed and stared as the old guy drew smoke into his lungs.

"Your man go?" he asked with a leer. The smoke curled back out of his mouth in lazy circles. "You should travel with me. I won't leave you alone."

She wasn't positive, but that sure sounded like a proposition to her. Damn. Where was the FBI when you really needed them?

"No," she told him for the second time in sixty seconds. "I'm fine."

"I like red hair. It's good luck." The man was staring at her hair as if he wanted to steal it.

He fumbled with the pump handle and propped it so the gas went in without him holding down the release. Taking a step in her direction, he let his gaze roam over her frame.

Reagan knew she towered over him by a good five or six inches, but he didn't seem to care about the difference in height.

He took one more drag on his cigarette and smiled a big toothless grin. The teeth that weren't missing had been stained dark brown. Reagan's stomach rolled.

"I hear you're looking for a man in a uniform," he said as he inched closer.

"What?" Her brain wasn't keeping up. Had she mentioned her father was in the navy?

"I saw a guy like that a couple days ago—over toward Backwash Monument country. I'll show you. Get in, we'll go." Before she could blink, his hand snaked out and encircled her wrist. "We'll have a party in my van."

His grip was vicelike and Reagan panicked. "No," she screamed, louder this time. She tried jerking her arm free.

Suddenly, a bloodcurdling cry came from above their heads. Reagan looked up to see what had made the loud sound. The scrawny man twisted his head to look up, too.

A large bird, either a big hawk or an eagle, flew straight for their heads. Sharp talons were all she saw.

She ducked at the exact moment the strange little man released her arm.

Seeking cover on the far side of Kody's truck, she couldn't see what was going on. The next time she raised her head, the man and his van were gone. But her nose was assaulted by the strong smell of gasoline. Looking over, she saw a steady stream of it pouring out of the pump and running across the parking lot.

"Let's get out of here." Kody's voice reached her ears. And then he was beside her. He took her by the shoulders and shoved her into his truck.

"Shouldn't we do something about the gasoline?" she asked as he started up the engine. "Wait. I've heard a spark can start a fire around gas. Don't."

Kody grimaced and put the truck in gear. "Too late to worry about that. Douglas is shutting down the pump from inside, anyway."

Her FBI savior slowly drove his old truck out onto the highway. "The Navajo Nation Tribal Fire Department will have to come clean up the mess," he said. "It's an environmental hazard. They have a special squad for such things."

Reagan's heart was pounding in her chest as they drove down the blacktop highway for a few miles. Eventually she noticed that her body and heart were not settling down at all. If anything, her blood was racing, fast enough to boil in her veins.

"Are you all right?" Kody asked.

She didn't know how to answer him. It wasn't fear or any kind of flight or fight reaction she was having now.

Turning her head to look at him, she caught herself suddenly picturing him naked. What on earth was the matter with her?

Reagan clamped her thighs together and clenched her teeth, fighting the odd sensations. Her body seemed to be in a terrible rebellion against her mind.

"I'm okay," she managed to answer through tight lips. "What on earth happened back there? Did you see that weird guy?"

Kody nodded. "I have to make a call. We'll stop and get some lunch and then we'll talk."

Talk. Right. Reagan wasn't positive that she could force herself to sit still long enough. Another bumpy mile or two, and she would not be responsible for her actions.

She wanted nothing more than to jump this man, who had saved her more than once. An FBI agent. Was she nuts? Had the fresh air somehow turned her into a sex maniac?

Opening her window, Reagan closed her eyes and fought for control. *Please,* she scolded herself. This is such incredibly bad timing. Don't let me embarrass myself by being that much of a needy freak.

Chapter 6

Kody found a booth set off by itself in the back of the Junction Restaurant in Chinle. It was midafternoon and the lunch crowd had come and gone. Two Navajos sat at a front booth drinking coffee, but the rest of the place was empty.

"Are you starved?" he asked as he waved to get a waitress's attention.

"Uh, no," Reagan told him as she shrugged out of her coat. "At least not for food."

"Excuse me?"

Before she could answer, the waitress appeared and they ordered their lunch. Afterward, while they sat quietly waiting to be served, her answer came back into his mind. He almost asked what she had meant by the cryptic words, but stopped himself.

What she'd said had sounded like it had a sexual connotation. If that's what she'd meant, he would rather not force the issue.

He was having enough trouble keeping his hands to himself when she looked at him with those big hazel eyes. Their attraction to each other was obvious, but it was not something he wanted to discuss. Nor act upon.

In the first place, he'd made that vow to the Brotherhood to remain single. Though he figured his vow had nothing to do with actual celibacy and wouldn't stop him from taking physical pleasure if he thought he could do so safely. Still, it was something to be considered.

His ex-wife was an Anglo from Los Angeles, and their relationship had been a complete disaster. Reagan was an Anglo from the big city, too. That put her off-limits as far as Kody was concerned. He just wished his body would agree.

"I've got tons of questions," she whispered. "Can we talk here?"

Slanting a glance at the two people sitting on counter stools, Kody said, "Maybe after we eat." He stood up. "I've got to make a quick cell phone call to the FBI office in Farmington to check in. Will you be all right for a few minutes alone? I'll just be outside."

Reagan sat up straight and frowned. "Certainly. I'm perfectly capable of getting by in a strange place. I'm bound to be safe in a public restaurant. Take however long you need."

Her disappointed expression made him sorry he had used the wrong words. It would've been much better if he'd let her know he believed she was a competent and intelligent adult who could be expected to act like one. That's how he should've handled things.

Under normal circumstances, he was sure she would have no trouble being accepted and helped by the Dine community. But since the war had begun, bystanders and outsiders were just as likely to be dragged into the conflict as the People. He had no idea how any member of the Dine would act at any given time. No one could be trusted. The terror was changing the mood of everyone on the reservation.

But he couldn't discuss any of that with her. So he just nodded once and strode out into the sunshine.

The first call he placed was to the Brotherhood. He learned that the man in the van at the trading post had apparently disappeared off the face of the earth. Not surprised in the least, Kody already believed that whole scene had been rigged by Skinwalkers.

Kody was glad to know, though, that not much gasoline had been spilled into the forest surrounding the trading post. The tribal fire department had saved the area from an environmental disaster. He was positive the gas leak had just been a diversion conjured up by the Skinwalkers.

Calling his FBI office next to check in, Kody got the latest advisory on the rumors of Middle Easterners. One had reportedly been seen driving an SUV off-road near Backwash Monument Overlook.

His breath hitched as he thought back to overhearing the guy at the gas pumps mentioning Backwash Monument to Reagan. Clicking off his cell phone, Kody took a moment to let the chill of the seeming coincidence roll over him.

Thank goodness for whatever invisible hand had sent the red-tailed hawk to the rescue. It had come out of nowhere and intervened on Reagan's behalf.

"You are welcome, cousin," said a deep voice from behind him. "Our comrades, the Bird People, were happy to assist. They have also agreed to search the rest of the day for the evil one and his van if that will help."

Kody spun around to find Lucas Tso, one of the

Brotherhood and a cousin on his mother's side. "The red-tailed hawk intervened at the trading post by your urging?" he asked, while clipping the phone back on his belt.

It was still tough for him to get past the fact that Lucas could visualize trouble long before anyone else. His cousin also seemed able to read thoughts, which was a little un-nerving for Kody's comfort. And now birds, too?

"Yes. The Bird People have come to believe that a number of their ranks are being infiltrated by the evil ones in the same manner as are the Dine. No longer is it simply the People against the evil versions of the wolf, the dog and the bear, as in the ancient legends. All living things in Dinetah will be involved.

"The Bird People intend to fight the blight crossing the sacred land," Lucas continued. "They have come to us for direction in restoring balance to the home we share."

"Do the birds hear the vibes the evil ones give off the same as we do?" Kody was fascinated to think that his cousin actually believed he could communicate with the birds. But Kody had learned long ago not to question strange things. Skinwalkers were the ultimate in unbe-lievable concepts for any modern man to grasp, and they were all too real.

But Lucas was much more of a traditionalist than Kody. He was the sole member of the Brotherhood who had never once left the reservation. He'd never invited the bad things in, like Navajos who went away from their home-land. Lucas had never contaminated his soul or his clan.

An artist, Lucas saw the beauty in everything and kept the Brotherhood rooted in their myths and legends—even though the rest of the group had managed to modernize most of them. "The Bird People receive the negativity," he told Kody. "But I'm fairly certain they feel it rather than hear it.

"I have said a prayer of thanksgiving that none of the Dine or Bird People were injured in this morning's skirmish," Lucas finished.

"Thank you, cousin. Explain to our bird neighbors that it would be unlikely that the human or the van will be found again in that form in Dinetah."

Lucas nodded and turned to leave.

"Stay for a few minutes," Kody called out to him. "I have someone I would like you to meet."

He'd surprised himself by asking Lucas to stay. Not positive of his own motives, Kody just went with the flow.

Turning back, Lucas raised an eyebrow in question. "Is this a person you believe to be a warrior working in disguise for the evil ones?"

"No. Not at all." Another surprise. Kody had meant that sincerely. Someplace along the line he had come to the conclusion that Reagan was not involved with the Skinwalkers...except for their unexplained continuing attacks against her.

Lucas agreed, and the two of them entered the restaurant.

Reagan tried not to stare at the two Navajo men sitting across from her. But it was tough not sneaking a peek at such magnetic and virile masculinity.

Kody's cousin was nearly as fascinating as he was. Lucas Tso had dark hair and dark eyes, along with a square-cut jaw and high cheekbones that could rival any fashion model's. But his eyes were warm. When he looked in her direction, his gaze oozed friendship and welcome—quite unlike the erotic pull she found in his cousin's deep, danger-filled brown eyes.

"You have questions about the People," Lucas said to

her after the waitress had cleared the plates and poured their coffee, and gone back to the kitchen. "May I try to give a few explanations?"

Reagan hadn't mentioned having questions. But then she realized that Kody must've told him about her before the two of them had come inside the restaurant. Or maybe the guy was psychic. She wouldn't doubt anything at this point.

"Yes, Mr. Tso, I—"

He held up his hand, palm out, and smiled at her. "Traditional Navajos prefer to avoid using proper names. That is your first lesson."

"Do you mean they don't use first *or* last names…ever?"

Lucas looked composed and calm. Reagan didn't feel at all nerdy for asking dumb questions.

He gave a slight shake of his head. "The Dine are given secret 'warrior' names when they are children, but no one ever uses them in public. And of course the People must use Anglicized names on federal and state government forms and in school. But among ourselves we rarely do."

Reagan thought that might lead to some very disjointed conversations. But she wasn't about to mention any of her uninformed ideas right now. She needed to learn more first.

Instead, she took a sip of coffee and listened to Lucas talk in his low, deep tones. Each of the Native American men she had met on the reservation seemed to have melodic voices.

But it was only the FBI agent's voice that could apparently turn her brain to liquid and drive fire through her veins.

She didn't dare look at Kody now for fear her new sexual awareness would get the better of her. So she tried to maintain her focus on his cousin.

As Lucas lifted his coffee cup, Reagan's gaze landed

on the silver-and-turquoise bracelet on his wrist. Carved
in a distinctive feathered pattern, it was truly beautiful. But
she'd seen that same design somewhere else....

Reagan slid a glance over to Kody's wrist. Yep. Half-
hidden under the cuff of his white, long-sleeved shirt was
a duplicate bracelet.

"I see you have noticed the bracelets," Lucas said, as if
he had just read her mind. "I hope they're pleasing to your
eye. I am the silversmith."

"You made them? Wow. You're an incredible artist."
Something about the bracelets seemed odd. Why would
they be exactly alike?

"My cousin is a world famous Navajo artisan," Kody said.

The sound of his voice drew her attention back in his
direction. Whoa. With one look her body started to hum
again. What was up with that?

Lucas set down his cup and slid out of the booth. "I
must go." He took her hand in both of his and gazed into
her eyes. "I'll leave you to ask the rest of your questions
of my cousin. But I will tell you that the design you see
on the bracelets signifies the wearer as a member of a
special group of medicine men."

"Sort of like the Masons or the Knights of Columbus?
I know they sometimes wear special rings or jewelry."

Lucas smiled warmly. "If you see this design anywhere
in Dinetah, know that you can depend on the wearer.
Trust him with your life." He turned to Kody. "May I
speak to you privately for just a moment before I go,
cousin?"

"Sure." Kody dug into his pocket and threw a few bills
on the table, then looked over to where she was sitting.
"Excuse us a minute. Finish your coffee. It's time we hit
the road."

Reagan managed a nod, but had to blink her eyes just to keep from throwing herself at him. This sexual urgency thing was getting to be ridiculous.

"The *bilagáana* woman lives inside a shell," Lucas told him when they were outside. "The nut in the middle is good-hearted and full of beauty. But I fear something evil is attacking her from afar."

"What specific kind of evil?"

Lucas shook his head to say he didn't know. "I advise watching her with care. Do not permit her even a moment alone."

"But—"

"You may need to contact a crystal gazer or hand trembler for a correct diagnosis of the problem. Your brothers will come if we are needed. But I sense that because she is Anglo, this is something meant only for you."

Kody thanked his cousin and watched him pull out of the parking lot in his four-wheel-drive Jeep.

Navajo crystal gazers and hand tremblers were medicine men and women who diagnosed the evil in sick people. They told the healers who were "singers" what chants, ceremonies and combination of sacred plants would be needed for a cure.

"Are you ready to go now?" Reagan's question came from close behind his back. "I'm terribly concerned about my father. Do you think that odd little man back at the gas pumps had really seen him? I can't imagine that my dad would actually be wearing a uniform while he was checking out an archeological site."

After Kody settled them both back in his pickup, he turned to Reagan, but had no intention of telling her the whole truth. "I have my doubts that we'll find anybody in the Backwash Monument area. That guy was probably making that stuff up just to see your reaction. And even if he wasn't, too much time has gone by since then.

"But we've got a couple of hours of daylight left," he added. "So let's give it try."

Reagan wasn't positive there would be any sunlight left at all at the rate they were going. They'd turned off the blacktop highway an hour ago and had been bouncing down a gravel road ever since. Her mouth and eyes were full of grit and her bottom was sore from continual contact with the springs in the truck's passenger seat.

The going was slow and she didn't much care for the way the canyon walls were closing in around them. It had started off okay as they'd played tag with a shallow creek that ran in and out of cottonwoods and grasses on their way into the wide canyon.

But now all that surrounded them were smooth sandstone cliffs, rock debris and giant boulders. Up ahead, she could see the canyon walls widen out again as the gravel road turned to orange-colored sand. Reagan wasn't sure sand would be any better than the potholed gravel had been.

During the ride, she'd been having a lot of trouble holding herself together. Despite the chill in the air, sitting in the same truck as Kody was making her sweat. Her palms grew damp and she had to keep rubbing them against her jeans. A trickle of perspiration ran down her neck and tickled as it dropped between her breasts.

What the heck was she doing? Here she was, knee-deep in the mysterious disappearance of her father, and her hormones were totally out of whack. She was lusting after a near stranger, and at any moment things could probably get terribly dangerous. None of it made any sense.

"I don't mean to sound skeptical," she said between bumps. "But do you know where we're headed?"

Kody grunted and kept both hands on the wheel.

"I mean, we haven't seen a living soul since we turned off the highway," she whined. "How could anyone notice *anything* this far down in the canyon? The sky has disappeared. It's so dark down here that you can't tell if it's night or just deep shadows from the high cliffs."

"The gravel wash is the only way in," Kody told her as he ground the truck's gears. "The ancient ones built their homes on talus cliffs like these where they could see unwelcome visitors before they arrived."

"But how could that man have run into my father here?"

Kody didn't bother with an answer as he drove around an abrupt bend in the canyon. Immediately up ahead was a sort of campsite, but it appeared to be abandoned at the moment. A long, narrow canopy tent was set up, and under it a folding table and four or five empty chairs.

He switched off the engine and they sat in eerie silence for a moment. "Looks like somebody's been working but they're gone for the day."

"Working on what?"

Climbing out of the truck, Kody again didn't answer as he bent to check the ground for tire tracks. He spread his hand out as a measure and judged that the really deep fresh marks were from a heavy SUV. The kind of vehicle that amateur archeologists liked to use.

Kody turned in a semicircle and spotted a narrow opening in the canyon wall behind the tent. If he didn't miss his guess, that rock crevice led off into a side canyon where someone had been working.

"Get out. Let's go up this way a bit and check it."

"In there?" Reagan asked, pointing to the opening as she climbed down from the truck. "It's really kind of eerie in that narrow alley." She straightened up, folded her coat in the seat she'd just vacated and narrowed her eyes at the dark slit in the rocks.

"Come on." Kody chuckled. "I'll protect you. Everyone is gone now, anyhow."

He locked the pickup and took her hand, showing her how to squeeze through the opening in the rocks. Once they were past the narrow entry passage, the side canyon spread out and sunlight streamed straight down the sheer sandstone walls, illuminating their way.

About fifty yards farther they found a series of aluminum ladders leaning against the walls and going straight up to nowhere. At least from their position it seemed they didn't lead anywhere. But Kody knew better.

"Looks like someone has found a new cliff dwelling. There aren't supposed to be any ruins in this canyon that haven't been mapped, but I'm betting that's what this is." He put his foot on the bottom rung of a ladder. "Stay here and I'll check it out."

Reagan put her hand on his shoulder to stop him. "No, please. You said yourself everyone is gone for the day. Let's just go, too. We won't find my father up there."

Kody turned and tried to make his point. "Backwash Monument is federally protected tribal holy land. If un-charted ruins are up there and someone is ransacking them, the tribe and the FBI should know about it. I won't be long, but I need to do this."

"Okay, I guess. But don't leave me here," she begged. "It's spooky in this tiny canyon. I'm coming up with you."

High above them, silhouetted against the clear blue sky, a large bird screamed a shrill warning as it soared on the last of the day's currents. At least, Kody thought it must be a warning, and his cousin Lucas's admonishment to keep an eye on Reagan came back into his mind.

But he was determined to go up the ladder, so he shrugged a shoulder and motioned for her to take the first step and lead the way. They would go together, and he would be her protector.

She took each step with no trouble. It was him, moving under her and watching her bottom sway as she climbed the ladder above him, who was having trouble.

He ignored his desire to reach up and cup her rounded, firm back end as her jeans stretched tighter with each step. For all kinds of excellent reasons, he meant to protect this woman. Protect her from the evil that stalked the rez. From her own lack of knowledge about the natural world. And most of all, from him and his outlandish and suddenly unruly desires.

When she reached the ladder's top rung, Reagan disappeared as she scrambled over the side of an unseen plateau. Kody was up and over the lip of the cliff behind her in three seconds.

Not being able to see her had all of a sudden made him nervous. He wished now he hadn't remembered what his cousin had said. Staying near would mean keeping their bodies in too close a proximity to suit his hormones.

Vowing he would still keep an eye on her, Kody also vowed to stay a discreet distance away.

Once he had his feet firmly planted on the rimrock shelf, he stared up at the ruin before him. It was large for an Anasazi dwelling, although it had been built typically long and narrow, along the fault line, and was protected from above by an overhanging cliff.

Reagan crawled out of one of the house's small openings, stood and walked to the edge of the plateau. "Just look at this view of the canyon." In ten seconds, she'd already checked out the ancient houses by herself.

Good job keeping her in sight, Special Agent Long, he chided himself. "In a minute. I want to see the ruin for myself. Stay where I can see you."

She ignored him. "It looks like rain. Smells like ozone, too."

Kody glanced at the sky over his shoulder and stopped dead. The clear blue sky of a few minutes ago had grown black and purple with threatening thunderheads.

"Uh-oh. That's not good news."

"You mean the rain? Why not?"

The faint sound of thunder could be heard in the distance, rolling over the Lukachukais Mountains. Kody remembered enough to know the lightning could be upon them in a few seconds. That was the way with the weather here.

"This time of year, it doesn't just rain," he tried to explain. "Storms over the mountains can bring lightning, hail, flooding, even snow at the upper elevations. Come away from the edge now, Reagan."

"But if the weather is turning bad, shouldn't we go back down?"

"I don't think—" He was about to say they probably didn't have time to go down the ladder before everything became slippery and beyond dangerous.

Just then a flash of lightning split the air and the clouds opened up in a deluge of cold, biting sleet, making the words pointless. He grabbed her hand and dragged her back under the overhang.

So much for maintaining a decent distance. It looked as if they were in for a long, potent night of togetherness.

Chapter 7

Kody lifted a hand to wipe raindrops off her cheek. It was a simple automatic gesture, Reagan knew, and not designed to illicit a sexual response. But it made her breath catch. She coughed, and her breathing came in shallow, raspy pants.

She shut her eyes, frantically trying to ignore the hunger pooling in her belly and settling with a thud between her thighs. What she felt was inappropriate, completely impractical and becoming impossible to ignore.

"No," she said aloud. By the time she realized that was her own voice making demands of her *own* better judgment, the word was already echoing off the cliffs and coming back again and again in embarrassing ripples. Reagan opened her eyes and groaned.

"Oh," Kody said as he jerked his hand back to his side. "Didn't mean to—"

Reagan shook her head vehemently. "You didn't do anything. It was just me…being an idiot. Sorry."

The setting sun threw gray spears of dusk over the craggy cliff, and gusts of chilled wind raced across the plateau, enveloping her. Reagan's overheated body reacted with a violent jerk to the dropping temperatures.

She started to shake uncontrollably and the skin on her arms and neck raised up in goose bumps. Every breath drew icy air deep into her chest.

"Can't we get back to the truck?" she urged, almost incoherently.

Kody shook his head. "Too dangerous now. One missed step on that ladder and…" He let the thought trail off, but the image he'd conjured wasn't pretty.

"How…how about using the cell phone to call for help?" she asked through chattering teeth.

He shook his head. "Between the weather and the mountains, we'll never get a signal out or in.

"You're freezing." He'd added the thought like a news flash, but it couldn't have been more obvious.

"Uh. Y-yeah," she stuttered. "I left my coat in the truck." She'd been overheated back then. But in the last few minutes, her sweat had dried into chips of ice.

It made her wonder how it could be possible for the blood to still boil in her veins as she stood this close to Kody. Outside she had chills, inside fire. Weird. And absolutely dizzying.

He took off his jacket, put it around her shoulders and drew her close. "We'd better duck inside the ruin—out of the wind."

Reagan let him drag her through a thousand-year-old stone doorway into a dry, windowless room. But once inside, she discovered it was still possible to see, due to the dull grayish light coming not only from the open doorway but also through a tiny hole in the ceiling that by all rights of physics shouldn't be there.

According to her calculations, directly above this room was a thick rock cliff. So how did that tiny hole get way up there through a mountain full of solid rock?

"These ancient ruins must've been designed and built by architectural geniuses," Kody said, as if he'd had the same thought. "I understand the rooms stay warm in winter and cool in summer."

His warm breath whispered along her skin. The words stopped making any sense and seemed only to add to her growing intoxication. Had someone opened a champagne bottle?

Reagan took a step in his direction, dumbfounded by the fizzy sounds popping and cracking in her ears. Absently, dreamily, she reached over and unbuttoned the top two buttons on his white shirt.

"What's up?" Kody said with growing wariness in his voice. "You sure you're okay?"

She drew her hand away from his chest, wondering what on earth she'd been thinking, to be touching him so boldly.

That was when she noticed her body had become hypersensitive. She fidgeted and grasped the edge of her T-shirt to hold it out from her chest. But as she squirmed, the silk of her bra cups rubbed over her nipples and made them stiffen. Every movement made her breasts more extended and unbelievably tender.

Sheesh. Her clothes were too tight against her swollen flesh. But they had been just fine a minute ago.

It had been a long time since she'd wanted a man to remove her clothes and touch her intimately. But that's what she wanted now. And she wanted that man to be Kody. Right this instant.

"Reagan?"

He was looking at her as if she'd lost her mind. Maybe she had. Her whole body was vibrating. The heat and the tingles moved through her belly, along her spine and into her chest and lungs. She was drowning in need, electrified with desire....

Closing her eyes again, she tried to force herself to concentrate on something else. For most of her life, whenever she'd been lonely or embarrassed, Reagan had focused on the calculus and trigonometry problems hovering in the back of her brain. But there would be no comfort in solving equations today.

"Something's screwy," she said aloud as her eyes popped open. "I don't understand. The numbers are gone."

Kody closed the tiny gap between them and took her by the arm. "What's wrong? You look…you look…"

The minute he touched her, Kody knew exactly what she'd been feeling. He caught the sensual vibrations through his fingertips.

Heat. The flames closed in around his hand and moved up his arm. He had thought they might need to build a fire to stay warm, but now it didn't seem important.

She touched the tip of her tongue to her lip and gazed at him with a dazed expression on her face. Kody got the immediate impression of sexual desperation. It turned him on just watching it cross her face.

He backed up a step. But he felt the overwhelming arousal as it crawled along his arteries to swamp him, invading his lower body and rising like floodwaters.

"I don't know what's going on here," he said tentatively. "But whatever is happening with you, and…me, we can't do anything about it. Not now, at least. We can't. Can you wait until we get back to civilization?"

Just who was he trying to convince? he wondered. Reagan didn't seem capable of making good judgments, or maybe any judgments, at the moment. Her eyes stared at his lips, unseeing. The tips of her nipples pushed out, stretching their cotton covering. She leaned toward him, absently begging to be touched and soothed.

So it was up to him to do the right thing. But right and wrong were tough concepts when every fiber of his being ached for just one thing: release.

How had all this happened so fast? Just a moment ago everything was different. He was the professional. The FBI special agent. The man who was knowledgeable about things like Anasazi and Skinwalkers. She was the pretty, if rather ditzy, genius mathematician, searching for her father.

His body *had* noticed hers. Right from the start. But the pulsing, thrumming, sensual beat had been simple to push aside, at least temporarily. Until they'd climbed that ladder and landed on the rock shelf at the ruin.

He had to stop and *think*. But…but…

Ease the desire. Give in to the compulsion. The words echoed in his head without his permission. They slithered through his veins and began squeezing out other thoughts.

Warmth suddenly didn't matter. Nor did food, water or even air. Nothing in the world could ever be as important as touching her, tasting her. Giving in to what their bodies craved.

Fisting his hands, he shoved them into his jeans pockets and took another step back from temptation. Somehow he had to find the strength to resist.

Damn his weak flesh. He had to *think*.

Through the haze swirling in Reagan's brain, she could've sworn she heard a deep, mysterious chuckle. It was a slight noise. A shadow of reality. Here and then gone.

But then a very real swishing sound reached her ears—loud and distinct, and seeming to come from everywhere at once. She looked around the room and checked behind her. It sounded for all the world like a woman in a satin ball gown, dancing through the dark shadows of the ancient ruin.

Reagan glanced over to Kody, wondering if the sound was somehow in her imagination, or if he'd heard the same thing. She'd been feeling goofy; maybe it was all part of a dream.

He pointed toward the floor, in the direction of the open doorway.

There, silhouetted against the cement-gray light of the stormy dusk, a black rope curled at the threshold. The long, smooth entity moved, slid sideways and blocked the exit.

"Oh my God," she shrieked. "A snake!"

This time there was no hesitation. No thinking. No consideration of consequences.

Reagan jumped at Kody, clawed at his shoulders and tried to climb his body. She had to get her feet off the ground. Had to press herself closer to him. Maybe even find a way to climb right inside his chest and hide.

He wrapped one arm around her waist to keep her from slipping. At the same time, her legs twisted around his hips as she tried to hang on for dear life.

"Don't panic." Kody shifted his stance to keep her off the floor and tightly within his embrace. "It's not poisonous. We've just managed to disturb the snake's winter slumber. He's not mad at us."

Reagan paid no attention to his words and tightened her grip on him while hitching her hips even higher. She buried her face in the side of his neck as he felt her whole body cringe.

It should be up to him to get a mental grip. To think, not act.

Do all the right things, he tried to tell himself. But when his groin tightened in response to the apex of her thighs pressing against the zipper of his jeans, he figured there wasn't going to be a chance to do anything right. Something, someone, had to give….

Rubbing her back in soothing circles with his free hand, he tried reasoning. "Snakes have to live somewhere. It'll go away in a minute when it sees we aren't leaving. How about—?"

"Don't put me down," she cried. "Please. Please!"

Kody's knees were flexing from the weight of the lush redhead's rounded body. Her hips were full and her figure was perfect in every way a woman's should be. But she was just too damn heavy to continue holding like this. He backed up to the smooth stone wall, leaned against it for balance and tried once again to soothe her with words.

"The snake's leaving, Reagan. See? It's gone. It got bored waiting and left to find somewhere quieter. So now you can—"

"No," she said, more quietly this time but with a more urgent demand in her voice. Her body relaxed and he knew she believed him about the snake leaving.

But instead of getting down, she wiggled her bottom, pressing herself harder against him and nuzzling her lips at the side of his neck.

He nearly bit his tongue. "Stop squirming. I can't take

much more. Get down now. Put your feet on the ground. Everything is fine. We'll be just fine."

"I don't…I don't want to get down. I want to get closer. I want you to touch me. Please, Kody."

"Do you know what you're asking?" He wasn't sure he knew up from down or day from night anymore. How could *she* know?

She shivered and dug her fingers into his shoulders in an obvious attempt to cling ever tighter. The prickling sensation of her biting nails set off his whole body. It would be so easy for him to forget everything.

Her warm breath tickled his skin as she groaned and said, "Yes. I know."

Chafing her breasts back and forth over his chest, she tried to make the point with her body. She knew. And he knew she knew.

But— "This isn't right, Reagan. We've just met…."

"I need you," she begged. "I need you to take the ache away."

Shoving her hips against his erection again and again, she stretched up and took his earlobe into her mouth, driving him beyond wild. She nipped it, then pulled back and blew a warm breath over the tingling spot, soothing the pain of the bite.

The tiny thread of resolve that he'd been clinging to disintegrated and dissolved, swept aside with that last breath of air.

"Dammit, Reagan. This is all wrong."-

Those might've been the right words, but his body didn't accept them. He leaned forward and settled his mouth over hers in a demanding kiss.

Wrong or right. Easy or hard. There simply was no choice. Kody would not deny her—or himself.

* * *

Outside the ancient ruin, the shadow of a snake slithered down through the craggy rocks toward a secret passage to the ground. Pleased that he had been able to put the right thoughts into the bright *bilagáana* woman's head, the snake snapped his tail with pride.

He had tried mind control for the first time back at the trading post. But he'd only managed to bring the two subjects out here to the ruins. Obviously that had been good enough. It gave him a second opportunity to wipe her mind clean and put the urgent sexual desperation where her own thoughts had once been.

Raising his head and flicking his tongue, the snake smelled the sexual musk between the two humans right through the solid rock. Joining them together in mindless sex was bound to bring chaos and confusion to the half-and-half lawman—and perhaps also to the entire Brotherhood.

And if the Navajo Wolf had been right in his original assessment, the snake would now have the power to order the white woman about the reservation at will, simply by putting the correct thoughts into her mind.

Hissing back a smile, the snake swelled himself up and made a dash for his hole. Happy to feel the Navajo world tilting out of balance, he thought of the Skinwalkers' major goals as they coincided with his own.

Money equals power. Balance is bad. Greed is good.

Reagan's body reacted almost violently to Kody's passionate kiss, leaving her breathless and stunned. She wanted to experience in the fullest way everything that was happening to her. Both in body and mind.

Hoping beyond hope to remember this sharp physical

need forever, she closed her eyes and tried to focus. But her usual clear head was anything but.

Somewhere in her subconscious, she gave herself permission to stop trying to think and to simply feel…just this once.

Kody's tongue rubbed over her lips, darting inside her mouth to dance past teeth and over tongue. His moves were abrupt, but exactly what she wanted.

She felt her body go loose with mindless pleasure when he sucked her bottom lip into his mouth, nipped it between his teeth and then lathed it soothingly with his tongue.

This was all so wonderful. His hardness pushed against her, and the harder he grew the softer she became.

Why couldn't she concentrate on what was happening between them? She wished to remember it forever. To use the memory during a future dark and lonely hour, bringing it out to please herself when the rest of the world ignored her needs. But her mind was simply refusing to cooperate.

Reagan fisted her hands in his hair and gave everything over to the kisses, though other parts of her body were starting to demand their share of attention.

Kody was beyond salvation. He turned them around and wedged her back against the wall so he could slip a free hand between their bodies. His coat edged off her shoulders and fell to the floor below them as he pushed her cotton shirt up so he could more easily reach her breasts.

Needing to touch…and then to taste, he worked his hand under the silky material of her bra and flicked his thumb over one puckered tip. Reagan moaned into his mouth and writhed wildly against his fingers.

"More. More," she groaned against his lips. "Touch me everywhere. I can't stand it."

He would've given a piece of his soul to be able to see her. To watch her body grow rosy and full under his touch.

To gaze upon her face as she climbed the mountain to orgasm. But the night and the storm had closed in, and blackness cocooned them in an ancient room filled with blind desire.

Kody followed his instincts and used his fingers and his mouth to give her satisfaction. He would have to let the erotic sounds she made be his guide.

Fortunately, she was very vocal. Every moan, every gasp spurred him on and reverberated in his gut.

Twisting and groaning against him, Reagan grabbed the front of his shirt and ripped it out of his waistband. She flattened her hand against his belly, then popped the button of his jeans and tried to slide her fingers lower.

Kody nearly bent double as he sucked one of her nipples into his mouth and tugged. Her response was incredible. Carnal and primitive.

He heard the zipper on his fly going down as she pushed her fingers against his groin. And when she reached his erection, palming it and circling her fingers around the tip, Kody's knees failed him.

Backing away enough to lower her, he pushed her legs off his hips and let her feet sink to the ground. She threw her arms around his neck and planted her feet while he spread his coat out under them with one hand.

"Hold on, sweetheart," he groaned.

In one of the smoothest moves he'd ever made, Kody pushed her jeans down her legs and ripped them and her new boots clear in less than thirty seconds. Pretty good for a guy who was operating blind.

But when he knelt to press a kiss into her belly, and breathed in the scent of her musk, it was as if someone turned on the lights. In his mind he saw her clearly. Every quivering muscle, every silky inch of skin, every intimate crevice.

Suddenly, the whole scene became much more personal. What they were doing was less about simple sexual gratification than it was about pleasing a woman he had come to care for.

He wasn't sure how and why things had changed, but when his mind's eye had recognized her body, his heart had recognized her spirit.

Reagan whimpered and pleaded incoherently for an end to her desperation. She dug her hands through his hair and dragged her fingers across his scalp.

Ignoring every doubt and question he might've had, Kody spread her thighs apart and nuzzled her mound. He palmed her intimately, using his fingers to smooth the way.

Finding her wet and swollen and ready for him to taste, he replaced his fingers with his mouth and gave in to his own needs and desires. With the first touch of his tongue, Reagan's body jumped and she cried out.

Her cries echoed in his head as he reveled in her taste. Losing himself fully in the moist satin of her core, he held her tightly, letting both hands cup her bottom.

Reagan's legs began to shake violently and her knees seemed to be failing her. Worried that she might somehow hurt herself in the erotic daze, Kody shoved his own jeans down and then lowered her carefully to his lap so he could keep one protective arm around her waist. It was time to give in to what both their bodies demanded.

Reagan hovered over his erection for a tense second as he fitted himself just inside her welcoming sheath. But when the tip of his flesh entered hers, her whole body jerked again as she shoved her hips down hard against him.

Her body seemed to have a mind of its own, reacting like it could not stand to be separate from his for another instant.

Ah. He sat perfectly still, letting her adjust to him and giving his body a chance to relish the tight, satiny fit that felt so oddly right and so…familiar.

But Reagan apparently didn't want to remain still. She arched her back and pumped her hips, calling his name.

He felt her internal muscles start to spasm around him. Needy and more reckless than he'd ever been in his life, Kody ran the flat of his hand up her belly and shoved the shirt and bra out of his way so he could take a nipple into his mouth again.

Tugging and sucking her warm peak with abandon, he let an electrified warmth surround them both. He grasped her hips and set his own pace, praying dimly that her pleasure would come along with his.

The slick motion became sweet sensory torture. Exquisite pain battled at the precipice of total bliss.

He felt her body begin its splintering climax, encircling his flesh and sucking him ever deeper into the whirlpool that was all Reagan.

Just then, and for whatever reason, Kody's lost sense of time and place came back with an amazing rush. Reality hit him square in the gut. Too late to save everything, it was not too late to do one thing right.

When he was sure her sweat-slicked body was finally beginning to go slack, Kody pulled out just in time, as his own climax put a shattering end to their mesmerizing dark dream.

Chapter 8

Reagan woke up out of a deep, dreamless sleep and tentatively opened one eye, only to realize that her arms and legs were wrapped around Kody's body.

Careful not to wake him, she lifted her head from his shoulder and eased her upper body back far enough to try figuring out what time it might be. If she learned the time, then she should be able to guess how long they'd been together like this.

The pearl-gray light surrounding them probably meant it was dawn. Did she really want to know that?

She was still half-naked and sitting on his lap, for heaven's sake.

Sneaking tiny peeks around the room without moving her head, she discovered the ugly truth. Yep. Apparently, they had spent the night in each other's arms. But daylight was making last evening's dark and shadowed frenzy seem more like a dream than like something that had really happened.

Kody appeared to be asleep, with his back resting against one of the smooth sandstone walls of the ancient Anasazi dwelling. His chest, with shirt buttons popped open to reveal a broad expanse of bronzed skin, had been lying under her all night like a bed. How embarrassing…and how titillating.

Flashes of what they'd done together last night—what *she* had begged him to do with her—sent both chills and fever along her spine. How could she have been so bold and stupid? And how would she ever be able to face him in the light of day?

She closed her eyes and tried to bring it all back, but it wouldn't come. Only brief flashes of the night could be retrieved from the place in her mind where her usual memories were stored.

These were wonderful, erotic glimpses of things she had never before experienced, to be sure. But peekaboo images simply weren't enough.

Swallowing hard against a dry and fuzzy throat, Reagan inched a little farther away from Kody's relaxed body. But it didn't take much movement to discover her legs, her *bare* legs, were entwined around his waist in such a way that it would be impossible for her to move without disturbing him.

Terrific.

"Are you getting cold?" The sound of his voice rumbled through her and the sudden vibration made her jump.

Reagan took a chance and looked up at him. His eyes were open and he was studying her face.

She hoped like hell he hadn't been looking anywhere else. The chills from thinking about their sexual exploits of last night had left goose bumps as big as chicken eggs on her arms and chest. And by now, her small boobs were all puckered and shriveled up, as if someone had thrown cold water over them.

How could she keep him from seeing her like this? Not possible. Sheesh.

"Uh…no. I'm good," she answered, hoping he wouldn't look down at her body. "How about you?"

Oh boy. The two of them couldn't just sit here making pleasant conversation and staring into each other's eyes forever. Sooner or later someone would have to make a move.

She got lucky. Without taking his gaze from her face, Kody tugged her shirt back down over her bare breasts and covered her chest. Then he slid out from under her as he brought them both to their feet with one slick move. He searched around for her jeans and flipped them over his shoulder in her direction, then turned his back and straightened his own clothes.

Something told her she had been more than merely lucky that it was this particular man she'd woken up next to. He was special. From the little she could remember of all they had done last night, he was *really* something.

Dear God. Why couldn't she remember more?

Scrambling into her jeans, Reagan cleared her brain of doubts and leftover mushy feelings and tried to focus. Kody had been kind to her on the way over here in his truck, and she'd felt safe beside him after the run-in with the odd man at the trading post. What else?

Making a concerted effort, she vaguely remembered suddenly wanting Kody with a desperation that was as foreign as finding herself stuck on an Indian reservation. The sensual urges had grown to be an imperative that for some strange reason she couldn't put aside. For once in her life she hadn't acted like a reasonable and intelligent adult.

Closing her eyes and wanting to hide, she distinctly visualized the memory of jumping him. Literally.

"Looks like the storm's long over," Kody said.

She opened her eyes and saw him silhouetted at the doorway, looking out toward the rising sun.

"I'm a little concerned about us being caught in here if the antiquities thieves show up early to resume their dirty work," he added without turning. "It's dry out. You think you're up for going back down the ladder?"

Out? "You bet," she answered quickly.

Because she'd apparently squeaked, as if she was in trouble, Kody eased his head and shoulder around to check on her. The growing light of day illuminated his facial features as he stood at the threshold of the ancient buildings.

She took one look at the strong chin and the crease in his cheek that looked almost like a dimple—and fell in love.

Which would've actually been funny had last night not happened.

As it was, Reagan didn't feel the least bit like laughing. She wanted to cry. And then she wanted to curl up in his arms and repeat all the things they'd done that she couldn't remember.

Dammit. Being such a good person and a kind man, he would probably oblige her, too. Despite the fact that he barely knew her—or cared about her.

Holding out his hand, he grinned. "Okay then. Let's get out of here."

Feeling light-headed and slightly groggy, she grasped it and ducked through the doorway. But once outside in the fresh air, she dropped his hand and moved to the edge of the overhang to stand alone in the sunshine.

Reagan needed to find herself again. Somehow, when she'd climbed this cliff last night, she had lost her mind. Maybe if she could recapture her normal ability to calculate vector analyses in her head, she would also be able to remember more of what had happened—and why.

Then she should be able to judge her feelings for Kody with a clearer mind. She simply could *not* love a guy she'd just met. It wasn't logical. No matter how sexy and nice he was.

Turning to climb down the ladder, Reagan found her ability to focus return as she hit the first step. And with the focus came lots of questions.

Yet with every downward rung, she became even more convinced that no matter what else might've occurred last night, it wouldn't change the dead-sure fact that she had fallen madly and irretrievably in love with a man she barely knew.

Completely in love. For the very first and last time in her whole entire life. What a typically geeky thing for her to do.

Kody sneaked a glance over at Reagan, who was sitting in the passenger seat of his truck. They'd been driving on the gravel road out of the canyon for the last hour in absolute silence.

But watching her start to squirm in her seat, he figured all that was about to change.

They had not yet discussed what had happened between them last night. Kody had no idea of what to say to her. He couldn't even decide how he felt about what had occurred.

Racking his brain, he couldn't remember ever before having had a woman jump him. That was something a guy just wouldn't forget all that easily.

Okay, so it had been one wonderfully gorgeous woman that he'd wanted to have sex with. But still, he didn't do stranger sex. Or at least he had never done it before last night.

Reagan was staring out the front window of the truck and absently chewing on her thumbnail. It should've looked like a childish thing for a grown woman to do, but it made her appear so vulnerable and lost that his heart gave a twinge at the sight.

As he tried to concentrate on the potholed road ahead, Kody's subconscious kept bringing back images from last night. Some of their time together was a big, dark blur.

But other things were as clear as a cold winter day in the desert. For instance, the way her breasts had fit exactly into the palms of his hands—as if they'd been molded to go just there. And the way her heady scent had been so familiar, as if he had known that smell all of his life.

Most of all, he remembered the way he'd felt when their bodies had joined. It had taken him a moment to recognize the feeling last night, but now it seemed perfectly clear. The two of them together made a matched set—not just single entities latched temporarily for pleasure.

Being with her had been like…sitting in front of a cozy fireplace on a cold night. Or like opening up a strange door and finding your favorite room on the other side. Or like…coming home.

For a few years as a young kid, Kody had known how good and right that could be, coming home to a place where everyone loved you and where you could always be yourself. But after he'd hit his teenage years, everything had changed. And then after his father died…

Well, the whole world had changed then.

Maybe most people wouldn't think that any of what

he'd felt for Reagan last night would be reason for a grown man to lose his mind.

But he hadn't. Had he?

Shaking his head, Kody gritted his teeth and held his breath, waiting to see what Reagan had to say. He still wasn't sure how he felt about her, but it might kill him if she regretted last night. They had been crazy and unthinking and they'd let their hormones run away with them. But wishing it had never happened was the last thing he ever wanted to hear from her.

"I think we'd better talk about last night," she finally said, still staring straight ahead out the windshield.

He gulped in a breath and nodded, but he couldn't seem to make a sound. Don't say it was wrong, he prayed. Having wild, savage sex with a woman you barely knew might not be perfectly okay, but what had happened between them should never be classified as wrong.

She shifted her body under the chest belt in the passenger seat so she could face him. "Don't you think we should've stayed in the canyon this morning? Maybe not up on the cliff, but at least down by the tent?"

"What?"

"Well, what if my father was actually there yesterday? We could've hid behind a boulder or something, and if he came back, we would've been there to talk to him."

Breathe. "Reagan, the people who have been working on that site are criminals…."

She shook her head and waved her hands. "Not my father. You don't know that."

He swallowed, noticing his throat was the driest he could ever remember it being. "Neither of us knows for sure your father was ever really there. But I do know that whoever has been working that site is doing it illegally. It would've been dangerous for us to be caught there when they came back.

"As soon as we hit the highway," he continued, "I'm going to call the tribal police and the special-agent-in-charge at the FBI field office. Let the professionals handle it with a real stakeout. They'll notify us if your father shows up."

She folded her arms under her breasts and frowned. "The numbers are back in my head."

Confused, he felt his mouth fall open, but tried to recover quickly. "Okay. Is that good?"

"It's the way it's always been," she said with a shrug. "Except last night."

"I see. I guess."

"Well, I don't," she complained. "I don't get it at all. It was as though someone hypnotized me…or drugged me. My mind seemed to be wiped clean…and then I got the weirdest, uh, urges." She took a huge gulp of air. "You know?"

"Sort of. I guess."

Reagan threw her hands up and shrugged. "Oh, well, you were so kind about the whole thing. You are a decent man, Kody Long. And I can't thank you enough for being there to, uh, take care of me."

Kody downshifted and put on the brake. "Hold on a minute," he said as he turned to her and narrowed his eyes. "Let me get this straight. You think someone may have drugged you? But you're not blaming me…you're thanking me. For what?"

Those slender fingers of hers started waggling madly in front of her face. "Oh, typical," she moaned as the tears filled her eyes. "I'm really bad at the 'talking to people' sort of thing. I wish I could just e-mail this to you instead. I'm sorry for being such a nerd."

"Hold on. Hold on." He took her hands and held them still. "Calm down. Everything's okay. We just need to talk it over."

She nodded and sniffed, but then waited for him to begin.

He held both her hands with one of his and threw the truck in neutral as he looked up and down the gravel road. No one was coming from either direction and he was fairly certain he would hear if anyone drove up on them. Where the truck had stopped was close to the main highway, but he knew the cliffs would echo any sounds and warn him in time.

Releasing one of her hands, he decided to keep hold of the other while they talked. To ground him. And remind him of touching her last night, and of all that had meant to him in the clear light of this morning.

Plus, while the two of them were touching, he could feel their connection. The closeness between them that he'd never known with anyone before now.

"Okay," he began slowly. "You are one of the smartest people I've ever met. If we start at the beginning, between us we can come up with the answers. Don't you think?"

"I suppose," she said in a slightly stronger voice than before.

"Good. Now when did you first start feeling weird? When did you, um, lose the numbers?"

She tilted her head in thought. "Those two things happened at different times. I started feeling a little strange the first time we climbed into this truck together." Looking up into his face, she smiled tentatively. "But I didn't lose my mind until we climbed up the ladder to the cliff ruins."

He knew exactly what she was talking about. The same things had happened to him at the same time.

"Can you define 'a little strange' for me? And by saying the 'first time in this truck,' do you mean the night of the killer bees?"

A reddish wave worked its way up her neck. Something he'd said had embarrassed her, and that worried him. He liked seeing a flush on her skin, but he wanted to put it there deliberately…erotically…not by accident.

"Look," she began as she tugged on the hand that he held tight. "I don't do flirting or coy. It's not my style, I guess you could say. Do you mind if I just tell you what I feel?"

Kody tried to rein in the grin that threatened to make him look like an idiot. *That's my girl.* He found himself congratulating her in his head for being exactly what he would've chosen in a perfect partner.

"Not at all," he finally managed to reply. "I'd prefer it if we could be completely honest with each other. We're friends now, aren't we?"

Had he really just opened his mouth and muttered that clichéd bull? Maybe she wouldn't notice. Or maybe she'd cut him a little slack because they'd been…close.

She widened her eyes and laughed. Then held her nose with her free hand and said, "Too deep, Mr. Navajo FBI man. I may be socially inept, but even I know a load of crap when I hear it. I said I will be honest with you. I really can't be anything else, but I'd appreciate the same courtesy in return."

He would not be able to be completely honest with her. No matter how much he wanted to get close and tell her the truth of what he was beginning to feel for her. He'd made a vow to the Brotherhood that he would never tell any outsider the total truth of what they were doing in Navajo-land. Their current mission was a huge part of his life, and keeping it a secret from her turned it into an out-and-out lie.

Of course, he'd also made a promise not to get physically close to any woman while the Brotherhood fought the Skinwalkers. And so much for that vow.

He sighed, straightened his shaky spine and bit back the words he wanted to say. He figured she would never believe any of the things that he'd been forced to accept, anyway. Not in a million years. He hadn't, until he'd seen it with his own eyes.

Kody let go of her hand and nodded in silent agreement with her request to tell only the truth. Even the nod was a lie. One he knew he would live to regret.

"Okay then," she said with a sharp nod of her own. "Then you might as well hear it straight from the beginning.

"I have only had one…boyfriend, I'd guess you could call it, in my whole life. I mean, I've had lots of dates, but only one…uh, all the way." The words were rushed and mumbled, but he got the picture. "And I never have understood what the big deal was about the sex thing. I mean…"

She hesitated and scrunched her nose as if she smelled something nasty. Keeping the laugh that threatened to erupt tamped down in his throat, Kody put his hand to his chin and nodded in silence. He sure as hell hoped he'd managed to look wise and thoughtful instead of being on the verge of hysterical laughter.

This woman was too cute to believe. But he would never want her to think he'd been laughing at her expense.

"When I first saw you the other night," she began again, "I…I just knew everything would be different with you."

Well, that pronouncement took a minute to sink in. Kody swallowed and tried a smile.

"Oh. No," she mumbled, sounding flustered again. "I never would've done anything about it. Don't misunderstand. I mean, I don't just jump men who look all yummy and sexy and everything.

"Or at least, I never would've done such a thing before last night."

Reagan nearly bit her tongue off. Was she a total moron? Where were all her smarts when she really needed them? She would have to find a better way of telling this if she expected to get through it without breaking down.

She began again, promising herself to sound more like an adult. "I guess I'd have to say you 'turned me on.' That was what I meant about feeling a 'little strange.'"

"Okay," Kody said. "I get that. I sort of felt the same thing about you. Not sure I would've used those exact words, but I do understand."

Taking her first real breath of air since she'd begun this explanation, Reagan relaxed her shoulders. "Great. Now then, about the numbers—"

"Yeah," he interrupted. "What numbers are you talking about?"

Terrific. After she told him, he really would think she was geeky. People rarely understood about the numbers. But she had no choice except to continue. She'd already promised complete honesty.

"For most of my life, I thought everyone's brain must work the same as mine," she began. "I've always thought in numbers—equations, numerical theory, some geometry… It's all just in there, you know?"

He shook his head. But he was paying close attention to every word. It made her feel good to think he would care that much about what she had to say.

Since he was so sympathetic, she decided to tell him more than she'd told anyone before. Perhaps Kody would understand that the only person she'd ever felt a true kinship with about the numbers was her father. Her dad had claimed to be the same way as she was, and she wanted to talk to him about it.

That was a big part of the reason she was so desperate to find him.

"I bet your dad's a math whiz, too, huh?" Kody asked.

Whoa. She hadn't even mentioned her father, and yet somehow Kody had read her thoughts. The idea that he could show such understanding and compassion was quite a thrill.

Then she remembered that unpleasant blank feeling from last night. And instead of being excited at the thought of Kody's understanding, she grew wary. Something or someone had tried to control her thoughts last night, either with drugs or hypnosis. It couldn't have been him. Could it?

Finally, she managed a nod. "Yeah. My father says his thoughts are all in calculus and geometry. I wish you could meet him. Maybe today we'll get a line on where to find him."

Kody picked up her hand and the same zing from last night seemed to race back up her arm. This time, though, she wasn't about to pull away. Curiosity drove her to find out why.

"We're going to have to get moving again soon, Reagan. But can you tell me first about when and how the numbers went away last night?"

For a second, it occurred to her that maybe he was fishing for some kind of confirmation that last night had been fantastic. Which, of course, it had been. But in the next minute she saw that he was just trying to understand what had happened that would cause a normally sane woman to lose her mind.

His question didn't seem terribly controlling. Just a genuine search for answers. She knew what that felt like, wanting to understand.

"I've been thinking more about that," she confessed, wondering absently if anyone else could talk and think and do trigonometry in her head all at the same time like she could. "It's impossible for me to have been drugged. The only opportunity anyone would've had to slip me a drug was back at the restaurant. But I felt fine and clearheaded, and the numbers were all in place for several hours after we left there."

She wasn't about to say she'd wanted to jump him for the whole of that time, too. But she had, even though her mind had been perfectly normal then.

"So when…?"

"The minute we reached the top of that ladder," she interrupted. "It was so odd. I was busy thinking about my dad. And about how the ancient Indian builders had managed to carve houses out of the rocks. And about the formulas they would've needed in order to site those doorways and smoke holes in the roof and make them weatherproof. And—"

"Hold it. You were thinking all of that, all at the same time?"

"Yes." And she'd been thinking about him then, too. "Up until everything stopped. And I went blank."

"When? Exactly? Try to remember."

She closed her eyes and concentrated. "The minute I stepped inside the Anasazi room for the first time."

"When you went in without me?"

Nodding, she opened her eyes but could still see the scene in her head. "Things started getting hazy from then on. But I didn't really lose it all until…"

"Until when? It's important."

"Until I saw the snake. But that doesn't seem possible." She looked up at Kody and caught his concerned expression. "I mean, I don't think I'm *that* petrified of snakes. Not enough to wipe my mind totally free of the numbers."

"Maybe not," he said. He dropped her hand so he could shift gears and let off the brake. "We're going back to my mother's house to get cleaned up and eat. But I want her to talk to you later. I'd like for her to tell you one of the Navajo legends while we're there. Will you listen with an open mind?"

"A legend?" Reagan asked. It seemed like a big change of topic and she was slightly confused. "About what?"

"Nature…animals. What can happen in the natural world when people lose themselves to evil. And…"

He hesitated so long that she began to fidget and wonder what he could possibly say that would be so terrible.

Finally, he put his foot on the gas, started up again and headed in the direction of the highway. "And about mind control…and snakes."

Chapter 9

The ride back to his mother's house was too quiet. Kody would've liked to explain the evil to Reagan so she would understand what the Brotherhood battled.

But his vow of silence wasn't the only thing that kept him from telling her the truth. She never would have believed him. At least, not without first understanding the history of the threat.

Reagan was highly intelligent. She would have no trouble grasping the concepts that had taken him most of his life to accept. But they had to be given to her one step at a time. In logical sequence, as she would say.

Walking into his mother's kitchen after a shower, he was surprised to see his mom carrying an overnight bag toward the back door.

"I have been called away, my son," she said, setting the bag down and turning to him. "I will not be able to

act as the legend teller for your young woman. I'm
sorry."

"Called away? Where?" His mother rarely left the reservation. It was part of her conditioning to remain between
the four sacred mountains that bordered Dinetah. Traditionalists believed that leaving the rez would bring chaos
and destruction to the family and clan.

Kody thought she blamed herself for his father's death.
His mother had gone off Navajoland when she first married, and had also agreed to Kody going away to college.
The idea of him leaving had seemed to bother her at the
time.

"Just to my sister's in Tuba City. But I'll be gone for
a few days."

"Aunt Naomi? What's wrong?" His mother was not
leaving the reservation. Still, it seemed odd for her to
abandon her home on an extended stay.

"My sister has been visited with evil."

Though he could hear the water running for Reagan's
shower, Kody gently took his mother's arm and drew her
near so they could keep their voices low. "What's happened? Is Naomi sick? Has someone been hurt?"

"No one is sick or injured. But they have lost half their
herd of sheep."

Kody knew what a blow that would be to his aunt's
family. Like many of the rural Navajo, they depended on
the herd for their livelihood and to keep them in balance.

"Lost? How?"

His mother's voice lowered to a point where he could
barely hear her words. "A hundred sheep and lambs
slaughtered. Torn to shreds. My sister says it looks as
though wild dogs did the killing.

"Your poor little cousin Emilie found her favorite

pets—with their throats torn open and their insides spilled on the ground. There was blood flowing everywhere."

Kody thought of his ten-year-old cousin coming upon such a horrific sight, and his heart constricted with sympathy. "I'm truly sorry for the Turner family. Do you believe it might be the evil ones at fault?"

His mother nodded sadly. "I fear it, yes."

He didn't like the idea of her going anywhere near there if it was Skinwalker trouble. "What can you do for them? It might be dangerous for you to go."

His mother gave him a frustrated look. "My son, the sorrow and the fear is great at your aunt's home. I go to do what I can. To be there for them in their time of need.

"I'll bring food and a shoulder to cry on," she continued. "And I will tell my clansmen about the strong medicine men warriors who are right now searching out the evil in our land. It'll give the family great comfort to know their emotional loss will be mended and that balance will be restored in the end."

"You won't say…"

"No," she agreed with a watery smile. "I'll tell the tale as I would tell any great legend. Without names or specifics."

"You think the battle the Brotherhood is waging will be a legend someday?" The idea was almost laughable. Imagine Kody Long as a great warrior and vanquisher of evil.

Patting his cheek, his mother nodded. "I believe that you, Hunter and your cousins will conquer the evil, my son. The People need you to be their defenders—even those who have no idea that deadly shadows are stalking their land, and who would laugh at just the mention of such things.

"But no matter what I say about good men restoring balance to Dinetah," his mother continued, "my sister's husband's clan may request a Sing to purify the land and drive away the evil."

"I wish life would be simple again," Kody said with a sigh. "At least that The People could continue with the old medicine, as if nothing was different."

Audrey Long drew herself up to her full five feet six inches and glared at him. "Life has never been simple for The People. It is the way of things. But holding on to the old ways brings the traditionalists comfort and peace. You know that. I have taught you about your heritage."

"Half my heritage, you mean." Dammit. He couldn't believe he'd said something rude to his mother, and he hadn't meant it that way at all.

His mom didn't seem angry with him, but kept her wistful smile. "Your Anglo blood will be of help to you in recognizing your enemy. Your Navajo blood will then be of help to the Dine when it comes to restoring the balance. You'll need them both, my son. Together they are what will make you great."

Him, great? When he couldn't even stop himself from being rude to his own mother? Not likely.

She turned and picked up her purse from the kitchen counter. "If my sister's in-laws, the Three-Who-Came-to-Water Clan, request a Sing, I will call upon one of your cousins in the Brotherhood to perform the ceremony.

"Help me out to the car now," she added. "I must go."

He nodded, picked up her overnight bag and followed her to the door.

But when she put her hand on the doorknob, Audrey stopped and turned back to him. "Do you want me to telephone our neighbor before I leave? She will tell the Dine legends to the young woman."

Shirley Nez, the founder of the Brotherhood, was a

next-door neighbor—living only a quarter of a mile down the road. She'd been Kody's medicine teacher and mentor and now she took care of the sacred plants that were necessary for the Brotherhood's battles. Kody knew she was a much better legend teller than he could ever be.

But then he suddenly remembered his cousin Lucas's words about Reagan. And Kody decided to call the crystal gazer instead.

"No, thanks. I'll call my cousin Ben Wauneka. Reagan needs much more than just the legends. She is being silently attacked. Perhaps Ben will be able to discover the reasons and tell her the tales all at the same time."

His mother's expression turned sorrowful for a moment. "I, too, wish with all my heart that our land was already back in balance. In time, I know, it will be.

"Meanwhile, take care of your new Anglo friend, my son. Defend her as you would a clansman. She has a good spirit and will help you conquer the evil."

"How do you know that?"

His mother just shook her head and opened the door. "I see her in harmony in my soul's eye. Years from now, long after I am gone from our land, she will be in the sunshine."

Reagan dragged a big-toothed comb through her knotted curls and cursed her red-haired genes under her breath. Of all the things she was glad she'd inherited from her father, the one she would've wished to skip was this rusty frizz on her head.

Ah, the hell with it. Giving up, she pitched the comb onto the dresser and dug in her backpack for a hoodie. Combing her unruly hair would not make her suddenly beautiful. So she would just cover it up instead.

Kody and his mother had no choice but to accept her

the way she was. It seemed strange, but Reagan believed those two people *would* actually accept her. Geeky ideas, frizzy hair and all.

When she turned the corner to the kitchen, her heart stopped as she saw Kody standing barefoot by the sink in his jeans, with a formfitting white T-shirt molded to his muscles. Water drops sparkled in his dark hair.

"Hi. How are you feeling?" he asked.

"I'm good," she managed to reply. Ohmigod. What wouldn't she give to be able to touch him right now? "Just a little hungry." She turned in a circle, searching for his mother.

He scowled, and the sight made the sunshine fade a bit for Reagan. "My mother had to leave on an emergency trip to her sister's house for a few days. I guess we're stuck, fending for ourselves."

"I hope nothing's terribly wrong." She had hoped that Mrs. Long would be the intermediary between them. Now what?

It was bad enough that she had to face Kody this morning after jumping him last night. But to have to face him in his mother's house? Sheesh.

"Things should be better at my aunt's house very soon. But in the meantime, I'm not such a hot cook. I'm sort of lost in the kitchen while Mom's not around. Do you cook?"

Reagan shook her head, but found herself smiling at the gorgeous man, anyway. "No problem. You've probably got PB and J around here, right? We'll be fine."

He laughed and the sound made her blood stir. "I'll have you know I'm a great connoisseur of peanut butter, and I'm most particular about my jelly. I hope you don't expect something fancy like blueberry jam. I only care for..."

"Strawberry," they both exclaimed at the same time.

"It's the only way to go," he said with a chuckle.

"Is there any other kind?" she answered with her own embarrassing giggle. "Except for Concord grape... maybe."

He slapped the peanut butter jar down on the counter and pulled a loaf of bread from the refrigerator. "Looks like Mom left us some containers of food in the fridge that we can nuke when the bread gets stale. We won't starve. And she made coffee. Want some?"

Reagan nodded, but his laughter was making her hungry for more than mere food. She'd better watch herself. How could she almost forget what had happened to her mind last night—or why she was here on the reservation in the first place?

Opening a couple of drawers, she found the silverware and took out two knives and two spoons. Then she slipped into the chair next to Kody at the kitchen table. They ate in silence for a few minutes, while Reagan let the familiar tastes stick to the roof of her mouth before prying them off again with her tongue.

"I thought you said your mother would tell me a Navajo legend," she began after a few sips of coffee. "Will you do it instead?"

Kody shook his head. "I called another cousin to come over and tell the story. He's a doctor and I want him to take a look at you while he's here."

"A doctor? An M.D.? Or in something more like the alternative medicine field, the way you are?"

"Ben works as both an M.D. and a medicine man. He got his Anglo medical degree at U.C. San Diego. And now he runs a one-man clinic way back up in the Chuska Mountains."

With her mind racing, Reagan sipped her coffee quietly

for a few minutes. "Why do you think a doctor needs to check me out? Are you beginning to believe that maybe I *was* drugged somehow?"

Kody took another gulp of coffee. "No, not really. Uh…you have to understand that Ben is one of the best diagnosticians I've ever known. He uses both modern and ancient medicine to *see* the problem and suggest a cure."

She heard the odd inflection in Kody's voice when he said the word *see.* "You want your cousin to look at me using alternative medicine, not Anglo medicine, don't you?"

He nodded before finishing his coffee. "Do you mind?"

"Not at all. I think it's fascinating."

Getting up, he put away the peanut butter jar. "Ben should be here in a few minutes."

Reagan hopped up, too, and rinsed the silverware. "I've been meaning to ask you again about that Navajo chanting I've heard you do a couple of times. You said you'd tell me about it later, but I think we both forgot."

He muttered a curse under his breath. He sure hoped Ben would show up soon. All this talk about chants and cures might be confusing for Reagan, and he'd wanted…

Wait a minute, Kody chided himself as he leaned his elbows back against the kitchen counter. Reagan Wilson could probably think circles around him. For that matter, around anyone he'd ever known. If she hadn't wanted to learn, she wouldn't have asked.

"Navajo medicine men are trained to use both sacred plant mixtures and ancient chants to cure patients," he replied. "Usually, they perform what's called a 'Sing' to get rid of the evil that's caused the illness or disaster."

"Evil? Is some of this based on a kind of religion?"

"Sort of. Sings are a big part of the People's basic belief

system, which I guess you could say is like religion. But it has a lot to do with the fact that our lives are so intertwined with the natural world. The plant mixes we use *are* similar to the rest of the world's natural medicines, though. It's amazing the things they cure."

Reagan thought for a moment, then scrunched up her mouth with another question. "These 'Sings' you medicine men use—do you think they work mostly because the patients simply believe they will? Or are they more along the lines of Asian treatments, like acupuncture maybe, that work on neural pathways that western medical practitioners just don't understand yet?"

"I don't know," he said, more frustrated than ever at not being able to explain things to a genius. "All I know is they work. And they have worked throughout all time."

When she raised an eyebrow at his statement, he scowled in return. Damn her superintelligence, anyway.

Kody wondered why she couldn't just be the sexy, alluring female that turned him to toast with just one touch. Why did she have to be so...

He heard a car pulling up outside and knew that would mean Ben had arrived. "That's my cousin. I'll go out and wave him in." Kody turned and headed through the living room.

"Why don't you wait for him to knock on the door or ring the bell?" Reagan asked from directly behind him.

He cast a backward glance and saw her having to take gigantic strides with those long, sexy legs in order to keep up with him. It brought a smile to his lips. "Ben is determined to return to traditional ways since he has come home to the rez. No traditionalist would ever walk up to a Navajo's door without first waiting at a decent distance until being invited in."

"Oh. What if you don't hear them? Can they honk to let you know they're waiting outside?"

A bark of laughter slipped from his mouth before he could keep it locked up. "Oh yeah," he teased, with more sarcasm than was necessary. "Honking would be *so* not rude. Just the thing for traditional Navajos to do to endear themselves to their family and neighbors.

"Remind me to have Ben explain about putting balance into your life while he's here," Kody said with a grin. "I think you seem to need the lesson more than I do."

"Well, I still don't understand why the People can't simply ring a doorbell," Reagan said after an hour, unable to stop her runaway mouth. "Do Navajos all have super-human hearing or something? I mean, what if you're on the computer or asleep?"

The corners of Dr. Wauneka's mouth twitched as if he might believe she was the nerdiest person who ever lived, but he was too polite to laugh in her face. "True tradition-alists seldom have computers," he told her solemnly. "Or doorbells, for that matter."

Reagan wished everything about the Navajos could be clear to her. This was one time when the numbers weren't any help. "Well, I can see how just stopping by might be rude sometimes, but…"

Ben Wauneka's eyes were almost black, much darker than Kody's deep brown or Lucas Tso's warm chestnut ones. And right now he was using them to glare at her. But she hadn't felt the least bit afraid or nervous by anything Ben had done so far, including this. She'd noticed he had on the identical silver-and-turquoise bracelet that Kody, Lucas and Kody's brother, Hunter, wore.

"Shush, woman," Ben said, as he let a smile soften his

features. "Give it a rest. Sometimes you must accept that doing things the way they've always been done is for the best. Being rude is one of the worst offenses in Dinetah."

Reagan clamped her mouth shut, but wasn't at all convinced. She shot a look at Kody. He'd been quietly sitting across the room, his face a total blank.

Ben began to put away his equipment. He hadn't needed to touch her during his examination, except to take her pulse and her temperature. The rest of the time he'd just gazed through a series of crystal cylinders and spheres as he shone a light into her eyes.

"Am I going to live?" she quipped.

Ben raised an eyebrow. "Were you in doubt?"

"No, of course not. It was a bad joke. What's wrong with me?"

Ben slanted a quick glance in Kody's direction. But his cousin sat stoically and remained silent.

"Let me consider it," Ben told her. "I'd like to confer with Kody later, before I give you my diagnosis. In the meantime, I promised I'd tell you the Navajo witch legend. Are you ready to hear it now?"

"Witches?" Reagan hadn't thought Kody had meant anything like that when he'd said he wanted her to hear a legend. "That's just superstition, isn't it? I mean, certainly no one can believe in those kinds of things in the modern world. Not really. I imagined the legend would be a story more along the lines of—"

At that moment, the still air was disturbed by a cell phone ringing. Reagan knew it wasn't hers. The darn thing had run down while she and Kody had been up on the cliff.

Kody pulled his cell from his belt and answered. Though he spoke too softly for either her or Ben to catch any of the words, they both waited in silence for him to finish.

When he did, Kody seemed irritated, or perhaps annoyed. "We're not going to be able to stay and listen to the legend, cousin. Reagan and I must leave now."

Ben stood as Kody joined him in the middle of the room. "Have you received bad news?"

Kody nodded. "Afraid so. That was the FBI field office in Farmington. They just got a tip that a known terrorist has been seen stalking the Dine College campus near here in Tsaile. I must go do some interviews there. See if I can get a few leads on the guy."

Turning back to Reagan, Kody said, "I didn't jump to a wrong conclusion, did I? You *do* want to come along with me? We may get some information on your father."

Ben interrupted before she could answer. "My cousin, you must not leave this woman behind. It cannot be her decision to stay or go. Not if it means leaving her alone. And none of the Brotherhood is capable of securing her protection. Not anymore. No one but you can help her now."

Reagan caught the confusion in Kody's eyes as he questioned Ben. But then she saw a look of silent understanding pass between the two men.

"What Sing is called for?" Kody asked.

"A Blessing Way or perhaps a Ghost Way Sing would be the preferable cure under normal circumstances," Ben answered. "But first, you must find the Skinwalker who is attempting to control her actions and thoughts. Stop the silent attack. Then we can try to heal the patient."

"Skinwalker?" Reagan asked. Had she heard him right? "What on earth…?"

Kody turned to her, but didn't answer. His face was unreadable. "You want to grab a coat? We may be gone until dark. You've got two minutes to get ready. We have to go."

"Wait a second," she said as he took her elbow and

swung her around, dragging her toward the guest bedroom where her things were stashed. "What did Ben mean? What was that word he used—*Skinwalker?*"

"It was nice meeting you, Reagan Wilson," Ben called from near the front door. "I have to be going. Kody can fill you in on anything you need to know."

She could hear Ben gathering up his things. "You will be well soon enough," he added. "In the meantime, try to fight the attack off. Concentrate. Don't let them take control."

Them? Reagan felt a chill ride up her spine.

What in heaven's name had she fallen into? And just who or what was a *Skinwalker?*

Chapter 10

Something was following them. Kody could feel the skin on the back of his neck crawl while he steered the truck down the nearly deserted highway through the mountains.

Ever since they'd rounded the curve on Route 64 and passed the Mummy Cave entrance to the canyon, he'd had the distinct impression of unseen eyes keeping track of their every move. But then, maybe he was just obsessing. In the first place it was broad daylight. And in the second, he hadn't heard any telltale vibrations.

He slanted a quick glance to the passenger seat, where Reagan was chewing on her thumbnail again, an auburn curl brushing her cheek. Kody knew what was bothering her, but he wasn't quite sure how to fix it.

"Why won't you tell me what a Skinwalker is—or what it means?" she asked after a few minutes.

He bit back a sigh. "Try not to say that word too loudly,

will you? The Navajo have a long history of believing in witches—a history normally told in stories, by the way. But at the rate we're going, you may never get to hear any of them.

"Skinwalkers are evildoers," he added with a wistful shake of his head, sorry that he was having to tell her in this manner. "They're Navajo witches who have learned to use some really terrible powers…in order to take control of the People and Dinetah."

And maybe the country and the world, too, he thought grimly. But he didn't want to elaborate. Kody could see she wasn't buying even this much of the story.

"That's… You can't mean you believe that stuff?"

Kody pulled the truck off the road and onto the dusty red-dirt shoulder so he could turn to face her.

"Look. I would've rather explained this to you one step at a time so you would have a chance to accept it the same way that the Dine who were raised here have accepted it." He checked her expression and still found that silly smirk. "But it looks like you are going to be forced into recognizing the threat whether you want to or not."

He put a hand on her shoulder. "They do exist, Reagan. I've seen them. Their legendary powers include being able to change out of human form and become animals…only these animals have superior strength and can do despicable things because they keep their human intelligence."

"Oh, *pullezz,*" she said, and rolled her eyes. "I'm an Internet gamer. I spend tons of time online playing, and I know lots of interesting plots about the same sort of thing. I kinda recognize this exact one, in fact. But they're *game plots.* Not reality."

He took a deep breath, put both hands back on the steering wheel but kept his foot firmly on the brake. "This is the very reason the Navajo refuse to discuss witchcraft publically. Whether you believe it or not, please don't mention anything—especially not the name Skinwalker—to anyone except me. It might be more dangerous for you."

"More dangerous? What danger am I in now?"

"Some of the Skinwalker stories and legends tell about the evil ones using other kinds of witchcraft to cause havoc and grab power.

"They're dangerous and have a whole bag of terrible tricks," Kody continued. "One nasty one they use is a white powder that causes disease and immobilization. Another is their ability to put objects into their enemies' bodies from a distance. That can bring pain, illness and even death. And worse yet, they're capable of mind control—making victims behave in ways that they decide."

"Oh." The corners of her mouth stopped turning up in a smirk and turned down in a frown instead. "Mind control. You think that's what happened when the numbers went away in the cliff ruin last night?"

"Reagan. Listen, please. Ben said—"

"So *that's* why you haven't mentioned what we did together last night." She crossed her arms under her breasts. "You think someone else was putting ideas into my head and made me jump you, right? And maybe that same someone's thoughts made me all hot and compliant, too?" Her voice rose with barely concealed anger.

The change of direction in her conversation left him temporarily at a loss. After a few moments, he realized he'd stayed too quiet for far too long not to be rude.

"You *do*." She turned her face away and looked out the side window. "It's written on your face."

"Come on, Reagan. That's not fair. I'm worried about you. Evil people are secretly attempting to bend you to their will, and I don't know why."

He never would've imagined her thoughts would go in this new direction. "I haven't had a chance to decide *what* to think about the things that happened between us," he finally admitted. "My life is complicated. And I haven't exactly had a lot of luck figuring out women in the past."

Silence.

Hell. Would he ever like to know what was going on in that genius brain of hers right now. But he didn't want to push her too far. Not about this, anyway.

Kody took his foot off the brake and eased back onto the highway. He stared out the windshield at familiar spires of copper-colored sandstone and wished he could find a way to make her understand.

His homeland had been forcefully shoved out of harmony, with ancient Dine beliefs turned inside out. And worse, the whole world might also be in danger from the evil ones.

It was his job to eliminate the threat. He couldn't just stop everything and work on his own problems. Or on hers, for that matter. Her physical protection had to be his only priority for the time being.

He sneaked one last glance in her direction. What a shame he couldn't stop now and show her what he felt about her. Words didn't seem to be getting the job done. And there wasn't enough time to find a balance between protection and pleasure.

But his body was betraying him, despite the lack of timing. His palms had grown damp and his skin sizzled with sensation. In his mind, he could only dream about drawing her close and letting his tongue and fingers do all the talking.

Reagan ignored the scenery as the truck flew down the road past different flora and fauna. She hardly noticed as gnarled gray cedars and purple sage gave way to the deep greens of spruce and ponderosa pine, or when red monkey-face wildflowers grew up in tangles right beside the asphalt.

Her brain was a jumble. Statistical analysis. Biological imperative. Maximum dispersible ratios. Kody's long eyelashes, lying softly on his high cheekbones whenever he glanced down at the speedometer. Random geometric patterns. Wanting so badly for him to touch her that her breasts ached from just thinking about it.

Hmm. Her thoughts were becoming problematic. She should be thinking about how to make Kody get past this whole Skinwalker business and go back to searching for her father. Instead, all she could concentrate on was how his brown eyes darkened to mahogany when she'd touched his arm. Or flamed with golden highlights as he took her hand.

The uncomfortable silence between them had dragged on for twenty minutes. All the while she stared out the window, only half seeing what was right in front of her. She knew they had driven past several highway marker signs and also past several tribal highway signs, announcing the location of roads or special monuments along the way.

But until this moment, she hadn't really paid much attention to any of it.

"Wait," she cried, breaking the silence forcefully. "Stop. We have to go back there. Did you see that sign?"

Kody slowed, just as a helmeted man on a motorcycle passed them going the other way. "Which sign? We're still fifteen miles from where we turn off to Dine College."

"That sign back there. The turnoff to Sheepdip Creek. That's the place my father's neighbor mentioned when I talked to him. He said Dad had told him where he was headed, and that's the place. The artifact cave is supposedly located there. I've been racking my brain, trying to remember that name."

Kody pulled off to the side of the road and stopped the truck again. "You didn't tell me the neighbor knew of a *real* place in Navajoland where we should look. Are you sure it was the Sheepdip Creek area? That's one of the places where outsiders are never allowed to go."

"Now that I've heard it again, it's not a name I could easily confuse with something else. Why aren't people allowed to go there?"

"The creek runs down into one of the spurs off of Canyon del Muerto. There's a couple of caverns hidden in the cliffs above the creek where well-preserved human remains have been found—sort of like those in Mummy Cave, but of extreme religious importance to the Dine."

"Human remains? Are we talking old or new?"

"Old. Very old. The ancestors of our ancestors."

"We won't go in those caverns," she said as she crossed her heart. "But we've got to get close. Please. What if my father is in one of those caves right now? I can feel it in my heart. We're going to run into him at any moment."

"Reagan…"

"Please, Kody. It shouldn't take us too long. I just know Dad must be right around the next bend."

Kody picked up his cell phone from the dashboard, flipped it open and checked the time display. "All right. I'll call the college and tell them we've been delayed an hour. But we can't go more than a few miles down the gravel road before we'll have to turn back. We can't get too close to those caves."

"That's great," she said without really thinking about what she was doing. "Dad will be there. I'm sure of it."

* * *

But twenty minutes later Reagan wasn't sure of her name, let alone her father's location. They'd been bouncing along on the potholed gravel, and with each bump electricity had been sending spears of sexual tension inside each layer of her clothes and skin right down to her bones, until she was totally consumed with the heat and the longing.

But she wasn't about to give in to this crazy sex thing again. Not when Kody had been so ambivalent about their last encounter.

She shrugged out of her coat and tried to concentrate her thoughts on what she was seeing out the window. They had traveled past a few houses, all of them set well off the road in the cottonwood trees. Farm animals dotted the meadows and stood under picture-perfect willows, drinking from the creek.

Reagan could use a drink herself. Her throat was as dry as the high desert, and her underarms were as damp as a swamp. It was typical of her geeky, *so* not cool style. Oh, how she wished to be like everyone else.

Sheepdip Creek meandered to the left after a mile or so, and Kody followed the road as it struck off from the creek and headed straight up a small hill through a patch of junipers and Russian olive trees. When they came to the other side of the grove, where the road was in clear view again, he expected to find the creek running back beside them.

Instead, he had to throw on the brakes and jerk to a gravel-skidded halt to avoid hitting an SUV stalled in the middle of the road. The driver's door was propped open but the seats were empty.

Uneasy, Kody backed up his pickup while still keeping an eye on the SUV.

"What's that guy doing stopped there? He's blocking the road." Reagan was muttering as she stretched to see from the passenger seat.

Kody narrowed his eyes and cast a quick glance over the scene. "I don't see anyone around." And that odd feeling of being watched was back again.

"How are we going to get past it?"

"I don't think we are. I'm going to turn around…."

"Look." She pointed her finger at an indistinguishable form lying in the dirt road right in front of the SUV. "Maybe it's someone who's injured." Reagan jumped out of the truck before Kody could put the transmission in neutral.

"Wait! You could be in danger." Cursing under his breath, he pulled on the emergency brake and headed out after her.

Protecting her was turning out to be tougher than he'd ever imagined. And all of a sudden the vibrations were beginning to reach his ears again. Of course. Dammit.

He was about ten paces behind her, but he'd never catch up in time. This whole picture was all wrong.

"Don't go any closer," he shouted. "It's a trap."

"Stop it!" she screamed, and pressed her fingers to her temples. But she did slow her steps, and at last stopped moving toward the danger.

By the time Kody reached her a second later, she was crying and holding her head in her hands. "The numbers," she sobbed. "They took the numbers away again. Make them stop. I can't stand it."

Kody wrapped his arms around her, torn between dragging her away and comforting her where she stood.

At that moment, out of the corner of his eye, he noticed a movement from the form lying in the road on the far side of the SUV. A weak bleating noise let him know the downed figure was a goat.

He threw one quick look at it to see if there was anything he could do for the injured animal. But in an instant Kody realized the poor thing had its throat slit and was tied and tethered to the underside of the SUV— Tethered with a piece of monofilament line that was almost invisible to the human eye.

"Hell," he muttered as he grabbed Reagan and took off running as fast as he could in the opposite direction.

Damn. Damn. Damn. He should've known better.

"What…?" Reagan lifted her head and tried to look back toward the empty SUV and the doomed animal tied to it. "Is it my father? Is he hurt?"

The supreme effort of dragging her away as fast as possible kept Kody from giving her any answers. He wished he'd had at least one second to decide which direction would be best to go, but it was much too late for that now.

Just as they reached his pickup, he heard an ominous click. With no time left, he dropped to the ground, taking Reagan with him. Rolling them both under the truck's cab, he covered her body with his own.

And the world exploded around them.

Heat. Flash. The stench of gasoline mixed with other chemical accelerants assaulted his nose as the ground shook beneath them.

But the pickup above them held together and remained in one piece. Luckily, it sheltered them from the flames and flying shrapnel.

By the time the worst of the heat had passed over, Kody was cursing his own stupidity again. He'd remembered to stash a shotgun behind the pickup's front seat, and he'd secretly stored his Glock in the locked glove box.

Great places for them to be now—when getting to them could cost Reagan's life. How were they going to get out of here without being picked off like the perfect targets he'd foolishly let them become?

"Are you okay?" he whispered.

He felt Reagan nod her head silently.

"We have to get out of here, Red. And I mean fast. But it's going to be tricky. Can you stay with me?"

She nodded against his chest again.

"Good. I think our best bet is the driver's side. There's a clump of juniper that can give us cover. I'll go first and open the door, then I'll pull you up and inside the cab. When you get there, duck down on the floorboards."

Her moan was soft, but he knew how scared she must be.

"We'll make it, Red. I swear we will. You trust me, don't you?"

For a millisecond she gave no answer. Kody began to worry that her mind was still blank and she would be incapable of helping herself out of this situation.

"Yes," she finally mumbled into his shirt. "I trust you. But don't call me *Red.*"

He took a breath. "Stay where you are a second. I'll be back."

Easing off her body and inching toward the driver's side, Kody found himself mumbling an ancient healing chant. It was one of the special Sings that Shirley Nez had uncovered in one of her great-grandfather's secret parchments.

Since the modern Dine language had not been written down until quite recently, Shirley's great-grandfather had determined that the stories and cures he'd discovered must've come from the special people in Dine early history. The Yei of legends. He believed the writings were meant to aid generations through the ages, but somewhere along the way, the translations had been lost.

While the old man had still been alive, he'd managed to translate only a few pages. It was just enough to give Shirley and the Brotherhood an edge in their war against the Skinwalkers.

Kody prayed that the particular chant he was using would work to fend off their attackers. But another big part of him also wished he had his shotgun.

Slipping out from under the pickup, he tried to glue himself to the driver's door of the dusty black truck. He wished he'd worn a black T-shirt today instead of this stupid white, long-sleeved FBI special that stood out like a sore thumb against the truck.

The running boards could've been a few inches narrower, too, come to think of it. But he was damn glad he hadn't stopped to lock the truck this time.

Praying aloud, Kody stood, gripped the handle and ripped open the door all in one jerky movement. Using the open driver's door as a cover, he pulled his shotgun from behind the seat, then dropped back down underneath the cab.

Waiting for some kind of threatening response to his bold move, he held his breath again. But nothing happened.

"You ready to go, Red?" he asked in a whisper.

"I guess so." She lifted her head from the dirt and pinned him with a pathetic stare. "Are we going to die?"

"No way." He reached for her hand. "A geek and a half-breed? Why would anyone bother?"

As he dragged her by the arm toward open ground, he heard her softly chuckling. His nonchalant joking seemed to be doing the job of calming her nerves. Just one touch of her hand had calmed him.

Two seconds later, Kody maneuvered the two of them and his shotgun out from under the truck and safely tucked them all under the dashboard. Slamming the door behind them, he reached up and locked it. Then he waited.

Still nothing happened.

He held his breath and listened. The crackling sound of the still-burning SUV brought terrible images to his mind.

But along with the images came a certain peaceful stillness. An absence of vibrations. Maybe the evil ones would not continue their attack. Maybe his chants had done the trick.

Trying as hard as he could, Kody couldn't hear anything that sounded ominous.

Perhaps...

All of a sudden he caught the sound of a truck motor, straining as it made its way up the hill behind them. Would this be the evil ones, coming to make sure their trap had captured the prey?

Kody couldn't easily move, crammed under the steering wheel the way he was. But he managed to shift onto his back, then point the shotgun toward the open window.

With one pump, he readied the gun. Gritting his teeth and concentrating on the window, he waited some more.

The truck sounds came to a sudden halt, seemingly right behind the pickup. Then he heard a motor idling and a door opening.

And then nothing except the frantic beating of his own heart.

After a couple of minutes, Kody thought he could hear vague mumbling in the distance. *Familiar* mumbling.

"Kody?" Reagan asked in a loud whisper from her spot on the floor. "What's—"

"Shush. Hold on." With great difficulty, grasping the

shotgun, he slid off the floorboards and into the driver's seat. From there, he was able to peek out the back window.

"Damn it," he shouted as he threw open the door.

He jumped out of the pickup and glared at the tribal cop standing beside an SUV parked about twenty feet behind the pickup—a local cop mumbling a Brotherhood chant.

It was the one tribal cop who just happened to be a member of the Brotherhood…and also Kody's brother, Hunter Long.

"What the hell are you doing?" Kody barked as he headed toward him. "You scared me half to death. Why didn't you yell or honk the horn so I would've known who it was?"

Hunter smiled while he pulled his radio phone from its place on the dash. "Didn't especially want to have a shotgun blast to the head today, brother."

"But…" He saw Hunter glancing over his shoulder toward the pickup—at exactly the same time as he heard Reagan opening the passenger door behind him.

Hunter's grin widened as he punched the talk button on the speaker end of the radio. "I also decided to wait until you invited me to come closer. After all, I am one Navajo who doesn't wish to be rude."

"You are so busted, Snake," the Wolf snarled. "I don't have time to deal with this at the moment. So far you have not made the slightest headway. And you're only managing to prove you are not worthy of the Skinwalkers.

"Our cult still wants to exert enough control to bring the daughter to us," he added wearily. "And it would've been nice to be rid of the Brotherhood FBI scumbag at the same time."

The Wolf glared but didn't wait for an explanation. "Instead, you detoured them in the wrong direction and then nearly killed them both. We want the daughter alive for now. It's the half-breed who can be eliminated."

"It was all his fault." The Snake broke in with a hiss. "But I did make her go to where I wanted. I *was* controlling her. Then the half-breed used some kind of magic chant that made me back off. It was beyond my control."

"Silence! Do not dare speak about losing control, you incompetent…" The Navajo Wolf lowered his voice and fisted his hands in the front of the other man's shirt, drawing him closer. "You have one more chance. Lead the white woman to us by controlling her thoughts. And do it within the next twenty-four hours."

The Wolf shook off his blinding rage and let go of the other man. "Then get rid of that Navajo FBI half-breed for good.

"But for God's sake make it look like an accident so the entire federal agency will not descend upon us," he added with a growl. "A car explosion? You are such an idiot. What were you thinking?"

Chapter 11

"Never again," Reagan mumbled as she swiped a hand across her gritty eyes. The sun was about to set behind the smoky-blue mountains as they drove through ever darkening shadows toward Kody's home.

It had been hours since the explosion, and she and Kody had spent most of that time trying to explain their version of what had happened to the tribal police and then to the FBI. But Kody's brother, Hunter, was the only one they had told about the numbers in her head being stolen.

"The next time I ever get the sudden urge to jump you," she said with force, "I will expect the numbers to go missing next. And I swear, I'll fight it. This control stuff won't ever take me by surprise again."

Kody cast her a dark look, then turned back to the road ahead. "Yeah. Great idea. That'll work."

"You think not?" She studied his profile for a minute

before it hit her. "Oh, I get it. You're saying you wouldn't mind me jumping you again. But it's a bad idea, Kody. Really it is."

She found the image as tantalizing as he apparently did, but didn't think that saying so would be too cool.

Kody scowled, and she watched as a nerve in his jaw began to twitch.

"I *liked* what we did." How could he not know that she thought their time together had been fantastic? "Don't misunderstand." Was he deliberately baiting her—wanting her to say how great she thought it was? How great *he* was?

Sheesh. She really wished she was better at these relationship games. Twenty-four hours ago she'd been positive that she loved him. Now…not so much.

He was a nice man. A kind and gentle man. That much was certain. And he actually *had* saved her life—at least twice. But could she love anyone this annoying?

The poor guy did look tired, though. His white, long-sleeved shirt would probably never come clean again. And though his black cowboy hat was back on his head, she knew underneath the dusty brim his hair was as filthy as hers was. She longed to be able to shampoo it.

That thought led to another. Them together in a shower. With the water streaming over them and then sliding down into sensual corners she'd like to visit again herself.

Reagan noticed a furrow growing between his brows, and she wanted to be able to reach over and soothe it—and him. But she was afraid to touch him.

As he remained silent, Reagan looked down at his wide male hands, that were, at this very moment, viciously gripping the steering wheel. Images of those hands touching her with gentle reverence and controlled lust dashed through her mind and played tag with her better judgment.

Damned if she wasn't dying to have him touch her that way again. Their one night together had been beyond anything in her experience. She'd never imagined sex could be that way for her. For a goofy math geek? Who would've ever guessed?

But it *was* just sex and not a real basis to build a relationship. Wasn't it?

Turning her face away from the temptation, she opened her side window and let the chilled wind cool her desires. It was well past time for her to start acting like the responsible adult she had always been. Scientific principles would save her life, if she would allow them to work for her.

And if she could find a way to keep far away from whoever had been trying to control her.

She glanced over at Kody again. A stray thought that maybe it was him who'd been trying to control her mind flitted in and back out of her consciousness.

Impossible. Judging by how he had let her take the lead that wonderful night in the ancient ruin, she was positive *he* would never try to control her thoughts—or her body.

Setting her jaw the same way Kody had, Reagan pursed her lips and made herself a promise. She *would* find the snake in the grass that was attempting to control her mind from afar. And then she would make him, or them, very sorry they had ever even heard her name.

The sun dipped lower in the purple-shadowed sky and disappeared beyond the mountain peaks. Somewhere out in the desert, she knew, the sun would still be bright and high in the sky. But here in the mountains the deep shadows of dusk were quickly turning sunset haze to creepy darkness.

A light chill ran up her arms. "Are we getting close to your mother's house?"

"Another fifteen minutes." Kody turned, checking on her with a quick glance. "Are you cold? Or are you starting to accept that night in Dinetah can be dangerous?"

"I'm not sure I buy into the whole Skinwalker scenario yet. But I am convinced someone on this reservation has found a way of using mind control from a long distance away. If that's witchcraft, then I guess I accept it." She hesitated a second and then decided to tell him her thoughts. "I not only accept it, I've decided to find that person and make him stop. I swear I will locate the bastard. And then…"

She let the thought dangle dangerously in the ever growing darkness.

Finally Kody turned to her. "You're still upset about the goat, aren't you?"

"Damn right I'm upset. It's bad enough I thought my father had exploded right before my eyes. But to use a poor defenseless animal as bait and then…and then…" She took a deep breath. "You'd better stick with me to make sure I don't kill the guy who would do such a thing."

"I'll stick with you, Red," he promised softly.

Reagan thought about telling him again not to call her Red, but changed her mind. It was the first time she had ever had a nickname. Well, if you didn't count the times she'd been called "geek."

And she kind of liked that he'd become familiar enough to want to shorten her given name. Red. Funny, it seemed just perfect for her.

It was quick and scientific. After all, that was the color of her hair. And somehow, coming out of Kody's mouth, it had an endearing quality.

She leaned back against the old leather seat and closed her eyes. Wanting a shower and a good night's sleep,

Reagan realized that her brain was tired, too. There were so many things she should be thinking about instead of the man sitting beside her.

Her father was still missing. And more and more, she was convinced that someone, or something, had either kidnapped him or hypnotized him the same way whoever it was had tried to do to her.

Dad was no artifact thief. And he sure as hell had not defected with classified documents.

Reagan swiped a hand across her brow again, this time pushing the curls off her forehead. But that would mean her father was being held against his will and could be in danger of losing his life. She had better quit daydreaming about Kody and start focusing on finding her missing father.

And she had better do it soon. Before she lost her one chance to connect with someone who loved her. And before she was once again left alone—for good this time.

Kody flipped on the headlights and pushed down a little harder on the gas pedal. He knew it wouldn't be dark yet on his mother's mesa, but he did not want it to be pitch-black when they arrived.

He gritted his teeth and vowed to start being more careful. Leaving both his weapons in the truck back at Sheepdip Creek had been the act of a careless idiot. It would not happen again.

Earlier today, while Reagan was being questioned, he had requested and gotten a temporary leave of absence from the Bureau. It was important that the FBI not learn about the Skinwalkers, and so far they had no idea. The Bureau's mission at the moment was to find out if a terrorist cell had really arrived on the rez.

Kody also wanted to keep Reagan's father's possible disappearancĕ in Dinetah from becoming public knowledge. Just until he could get more information.

He had to be free to give Reagan complete protection and also help in the search for her father. A leave would make it much easier for him to do things his way. He was counting on the Brotherhood to back him up.

Sneaking a glance at Reagan, he absently patted the Glock, which was now residing in his shoulder holster where it belonged. He could understand how tired she must be. Her clothes were a mess and tiny stress lines had appeared at the corners of her eyes.

Man, what he wouldn't give to be able to fold her into his arms and protect her from everything. To smooth those lines away, rocking her into a peaceful sleep. All he wanted to do was keep the evil ones—and those mental ghosts of hers—at a safe distance.

He wasn't too sure why he felt that way. But she had to be protected.

Reagan was so much more than she knew. So much more than he could ever be worthy of keeping.

Her questions this morning about what he'd thought of their experience together had taken him by surprise. But in the back of his mind, he'd been trying to figure it out for himself ever since.

He knew she had been asking about his emotional response to her, and not just about the sex. The sex was great. Beyond great. But emotions weren't something he'd ever let himself think about.

Of course, he *had* experienced a few emotional responses in the past. Loneliness. Fear. Overwhelming sadness when his father had died.

Mulling over those for a second, Kody realized he had

left out one big emotion—love. He narrowed his eyes and thought about it some more.

Love was the most difficult emotion to get a handle on. If you let yourself love someone too much, it also hurt too much when that love went away.

His father's death had nearly killed him. Since then, he had held back his love for the rest of his family. He respected and cared for his mother and his brother, but never again would he allow himself to be consumed by love—for anyone.

As a matter of fact, now that he thought about it, he had never actually opened up and allowed himself to love his ex-wife. He'd always imagined it had been Marsha who had never loved him. She'd divorced him, after all.

But in truth, he had probably hurt her by not giving the kind of love that a wife deserved. The kind of love she'd had a right to expect.

Sighing, Kody shook the images from his head. Too much internalizing could be hurtful. And his thoughts were becoming downright depressing. Enough of that.

He needed to keep his mind clear and his thoughts focused where they belonged. On the evil ones and on how to protect Reagan while still trying to locate her father.

Pulling into his mother's gravel drive and heading up the hill, Kody wondered if he should begin again with Reagan. He must learn to remain professional and to distance himself from all her distractions.

Letting himself go, as he had the other night, was not the way to win this war with the evil ones. He could *not* allow himself to think about Reagan too much.

From now on, he would stick to being her protector. As he parked the pickup, surrounded by the last vestiges of ice-blue dusk, he made another vow—to be a first-rate member of the Brotherhood. And nothing more.

* * *

Reagan paced up and down in Mrs. Long's kitchen and concentrated on different aspects of the problem. So many separate things were going through her mind at once that she felt like a computer router, directing each thought to its own special place in her brain.

Some pieces fit into the puzzle, other pieces seemed to come from an entirely different picture. As usual in new scientific dilemmas, she needed more information in order to draw a hypothesis.

"Feeling better?" The sound of Kody's voice behind her made her shoulders straighten and the corners of her mouth lift up in a special smile just for him.

"Yes," she said as she swung around. "But I was thinking that I needed my…"

Her mouth dropped open and her words died in her throat. She was unaccustomed to facing a virile man half-dressed and fresh from his shower. A man who made her bones rattle and her teeth tingle with ultrasensitivity whenever he looked in her direction.

Right now, he was staring at her like she was a glass of wine and he had been on the wagon for years. Her mouth open, she gulped in air and tried to get past the fact that he didn't have a shirt on.

His hair was slicked back and dripping water on his bare skin. Water ran in rivulets down his shoulders, across gleaming chest muscles and down his flat stomach, disappearing past the open top button of his jeans.

Stunned by the sudden desire to let her fingers capture the water, or maybe by the need to lick the droplets away as she put her mouth where the rivulets flowed, Reagan just stood there gawking. Her mind went blank. But she was absolutely sure no one was trying to control her this time.

No indeed. This was just her own naiveté and foolishness, desiring something that should be forbidden.

Swallowing once, she opened her mouth again, but no words could get past the lump in her throat. She swallowed once more.

"Um…what was I saying?" She waited a second for him to answer, but his eyes stayed focused on her mouth and he never moved a muscle. "Oh yeah. I need access to the Internet. A few things are bothering me. Some loose ends. And I can't come up with decent theories without all the postulates."

He finally managed to drag his eyes away from her with a shake of his head. It made her wonder if he'd been feeling some force controlling him, too.

"Won't your handheld wireless do? Is it still in your jacket pocket?" He moved to the sink and poured himself a glass of water, keeping his back to her.

"Batteries are dead. I've plugged it into the recharger. But the thing was so totally gone it'll take hours for it to come back up. Your mother doesn't have a computer at all?"

Reagan had sneaked a look around while he was in the shower. But now she wished she hadn't just admitted to being a snoop.

Kody turned and flashed her a smile. "Maybe if you bounce some of your ideas off me, together we can come up with a few answers. Are you hungry?"

"I could eat." Though she'd said the words in her best casual manner, her stomach growled right at that moment.

Kody raised an eyebrow. "Yeah, I guess you could. Neither of us has had anything since breakfast. Let's nuke one of mom's containers of food. And I can cook fry bread to go with it. She taught me how. Sit down. It should be ready in a few minutes."

Pulling out one of the heavy kitchen chairs, Reagan considered which of the many thoughts in her head she wanted to talk to him about. There were a couple of things she had no intention of saying. Questions she would rather find answers to on her own. Those would wait for her Blackberry to come back up.

He set two big bowls of steaming stew down on the table right before he flipped the bread off the electric griddle and onto a plate. "Here you go."

"What is the soupy stuff your mom made?"

"Stew."

"Yes, but what kind of stew?"

"Mutton."

"Oh." She decided to shut up and eat. She couldn't think about sheep becoming stew meat right now. Not when thoughts of sheep could so easily turn to thoughts of goats. And thoughts of goats could so easily turn to one in par-ticular….

Sheesh. "Pass the bread, please."

Twenty minutes later, when she had eaten her fill of bread and fruit and one bite of stew, she got up and began running water for their dishes.

She kept her back to Kody, who was drinking a last cup of after-dinner coffee. It was much easier to talk to him when she couldn't see his eyes.

"So, what kinds of things have you been thinking about?" he asked before she could even begin.

"You sound like a cop. Don't push, please," she began. "I have what seems like dozens of bits of information rumbling around in my head. And I'm trying to pull out one strand that actually makes sense. But I don't know what you can do to help me."

"Why not just start talking? Maybe something will resonate in our collective consciousness."

"That isn't the way I normally solve problems—by talking, that is. I usually flit around online until something clicks."

"Just try it."

She turned her head to look at him, but wished she hadn't. No matter that the sound of his voice had been soft and professional, she discovered that behind her back he had been touching her body with his eyes. Gently, to be sure. But with a tremendous promise of something hotter and more sensual under that.

Whipping her head back around to the dishes in the sink, she said the first thing that tripped out of her mouth. "Who would kidnap my father? And please don't start with the Skinwalkers again. I have a feeling you know something you aren't telling me."

"Why do you think your father has been kidnapped?"

"Just putting pieces together. If he hadn't been taken against his will somehow, he would've contacted me by now. And that whole scenario of him defecting with classified plans sounds phony. So what do you know that I don't?"

Her question was met by a long silence. It took everything she had not to turn around to see what expression Kody would be wearing this time.

"I know that a Middle Eastern terrorist cell is rumored to be on the reservation," he finally admitted. "The Bureau hasn't been able to pin down the truth or there would be hundreds of agents swarming over the rez by now. But I understand the leader of one particular group has let it be known over the Internet that he would pay hundreds of millions for certain, uh, military goods and services."

That news was incredible and confusing, so she turned

to question Kody. "Like guns, or what? Uranium waste material? Nuclear plans? What?"

"Something classified," he answered warily. "But the Bureau learned from the CIA that this particular rumor was about a terrorist cell a little more sophisticated than most. They may have found a covert way into the U.S. through the Mexican border.

"On the other hand," he added, "I've been wondering why a sophisticated group like that would even consider coming anyplace so remote and seemingly useless to them as the Navajo Four Corners reservation. We can barely scrape together enough to feed all our people. So what would they find so valuable out here?"

Kody shifted his chair and leaned back, crossing one ankle at the knee. "I don't know what project your old man was working on, Red. But I'm half surprised it wasn't *you* they were looking for instead of him."

Reagan stood there gaping at him for a moment, trying to put more of the pieces into order. "You think my father has been kidnapped by some group, don't you?"

He nodded but kept silent.

"I need to notify someone," she said in haste. "I should go to my father's C.O. Or I should call the…" She paused, feeling as if she'd just run out of steam. No one would believe her. Besides, there was something else niggling at her brain. Something still not on track.

"Maybe I should leave here," she muttered at last. "Go far away from you. Whoever took my father obviously knows where I am. Your life is probably in danger every minute we're together."

"Would you leave the rez altogether? Go back to California? Leave, not knowing what really happened to your father?"

"No, of course not." She was suddenly fuming. Furious at the situation and furious at her own inability to concentrate on the problem at hand.

Kody moved as fast as a shadow and ended up standing beside her, violating her space, before she could object. "Thanks for trying to protect me, Red. But you're not going anywhere in Dinetah without me to watch your back."

His warm, callused fingers brushed her cheek, and alarm bells began ringing in her head. That first touch was electric—and tender. But she was afraid of it, of him. Of what there was between them that she didn't understand.

She tried inching away. "My head is still full of questions. Like how would Middle Easterners manage to capture my father? And who has been trying to control my mind? And…and…" Kody had better move back soon. Her knees were getting weaker and she saw the hunger growing in his eyes.

"And what happened to you that you think you have no luck with women," she blurted. "And…" Oops. That was definitely not what she'd meant to say.

Kody didn't seem to take notice of anything she had been saying. He gently cupped her face in both his hands and whispered a question of his own. "Are the numbers still all in place?"

Mesmerized by his dark eyes, she could only nod.

"Good," he murmured against her lips. "Let's see if we can manage to blank them out—all by ourselves."

Chapter 12

Ａs much as Kody needed Reagan right now, he was afraid to push her too hard. Sometimes she looked so fragile.

But he knew about the sensual creature that lurked inside Reagan Wilson. And knowing was making him crazy.

He'd seen it. Seen for himself on their insane night in the ruin that she had more power and strength of spirit than she could possibly know. Even with the evil ones trying to control her mind, her own potent force had shone right through the darkness.

Kody felt compelled to bring that out in her one more time. Was he selfish? Because in truth her strength turned him on almost more than he could handle.

No. He just had to see it again. Had to have that power under him, surrounding him. He craved it, with both body and spirit.

The silken lips he'd been fantasizing about were only

a whisper away. Right here, right now. He closed the gap, feeling more aroused than he could ever remember.

Their kiss began as a reverent touch of lips. But when she opened her mouth and he heard a moan coming from deep inside her body, Kody lost whatever was left of his control.

He deepened the kiss, using his tongue as a token, a symbol of his need to sweep aside her fears. He tasted. Drank from the honey that was all Reagan.

And then he slipped beyond all redemption. He didn't lose it from any form of mind control, but from the power of the sweetness and harmony he'd found in her embrace.

Kody felt her trembling and growing weak-kneed. Wrapping his arm around her waist protectively, he fitted her body to his own. The match was perfect, as he'd remembered. She was his other half. Just as if she'd been created specifically to be that one spark he'd felt had been missing from his life.

"Touch me," she urged in a hoarse whisper. "Please, Kody. I want…"

Smiling, he placed his lips in the hollow between her shoulder and her neck, and at the first contact, she arched and groaned. It made him nuts. Crazed by the taste of warm skin and by the idea of what he could do to her by using his lips and teeth.

With most of his mind on her sweet thighs and the even sweeter spot between them, Kody gave way to the blood gushing through his veins, pumping hot and thick and pooling in his groin.

Greedy, and with the lust rising to impossible heights inside him, he drew her closer. He felt her pulse quicken in response to his openmouthed kisses.

She pressed her hips against his groin and moaned.

Kody grew harder and heavier with her every move. He cupped her bottom and tipped her pelvis up, fitting the two of them together.

She gasped softly and pushed her upper body away from him. For one second he was struck by complete panic, knowing if she told him no, he would have to accept it immediately.

But…*please don't say no.*

Apparently it wasn't no Reagan had meant when she'd leaned back. Her hands were busily moving over his chest, up his shoulders and down his arms. It seemed she simply had to touch his skin the same as he had needed to feel hers.

He studied her heavy-lidded eyes and found her mesmerized by the way his chest muscles reacted, tightening under her palms.

Barely able to stand the sight of her like that, he knew he might collapse if he couldn't touch her in return. She was wearing a soft sweatshirt that ended just above the rolled waistband of her sweatpants. It was a perfect spot for a caress.

Kody bent to put his mouth just there, but soon gave up and ripped the shirt over her head in a ferocious move. Suddenly naked from the waist up, she went rigid, her arms going to her sides like a little tin soldier.

"Aw, Red. It's okay. Better than okay. Trust me." *Dearest one, please, please trust me,* he silently begged.

Moving closer, he gently cupped the small globes of her breasts. They fit into his hands perfectly and seemed to be growing fuller and more peaked as he watched. Bending his head, he took one tip into his mouth, wishing he could both see and taste in unison.

She was beautiful. And tasted like nectar, all sweet and salty at the same time.

Kissing and lathing her hardened nipple, he almost

missed the way her hands were tugging at his shoulders, urging him closer. Urging him to take her.

And take her he did. With one swoop, he lifted her in his arms and moved to the nearest comfortable surface he could find—his own, long-ago bed.

He set her down on her feet right next to it. *One,* he counted absently as he ripped off his jeans. *Two,* he mentally added as he jerked her sweatpants down and shoved them out of the way.

By the count of three, Reagan had flung herself backward on the bed and raised her arms, begging him with motions and mumbled words to come closer. She had most definitely not changed her mind.

He didn't care at all if she lost control now. Not as long as he could go with her.

But there was one more thing he thought he should do first. He would've crossed his fingers for luck if he'd had a free hand. But instead, he used both hands to pull open the bottom drawer on the bedside stand, then dug under a stack of handkerchiefs for the foil packets he had secreted there years ago. The damn condoms might be too old to work, but anything was better than nothing.

Flipping a couple packets onto the tabletop, Kody turned back to Reagan, who was writhing on the bed beside him. She was truly beautiful. So beautiful that he just had to watch her.

He used both his palms to stroke her skin, moving from her neck down to massage her breasts. Mmm. Warm, silken and sensitive. The tips responded to his touch once again, so he bent over to take one into his mouth. He drew her in, sucked hard, then used the flat of his tongue to lathe the tip.

Reagan moaned and arched her hips. Kody almost

laughed. Her body was begging him to bring her to release in the exact same way his own was thumping and pushing for him to get on with it.

To please them both, he tried to set a slower pace. He wanted to see what kind of reactions Reagan would make to his caresses now that she was in complete control of her mind.

He laid his hands flat on her quivering belly and stroked around her navel. The skin was so soft, so tantalizing. Her hips came up and off the bed again as she arched her back and urged him to hurry.

"Easy, Red. We'll get there." He let his hands glide over her hips to cup her round, naked bottom. The minute he grasped her flesh and squeezed, her thighs fell apart in an open invitation.

"Now…now…*Kody*…"

He smiled at her again, even though he was barely able to breathe as the loud thumping of his heart left his chest and leapt right into his throat, choking him with emotions he had never before acknowledged.

"Wait," he said with a rasp.

One of his blind dreams from the other night had been of the delicate skin on the inside of her thighs. He looked down her body to see in the light what he remembered seeing in his mind's eye that night in pitch darkness. Yeah. Satin skin, quivering and pulsating, awaiting his touch.

He inched back, just enough to let his tongue glide up from the inside of her knee to the slick center of her sensation. He knew the spot; it lay just under a rusty cover of fur. The first taste of her honey held such promise he nearly lost his mind and stayed to drink too long.

But Reagan didn't lose *her* mind. In fact, she found the power of control at last. That strength of will that he had already visualized while they had been in the darkness of the ancient room.

She screamed something incoherently, bolted out from under him and grabbed up one of the packets, ripping the foil with her teeth.

When she reached out for him, he knew it would be too much to have her touch him now. Kody tore the protection from her hand and slipped it over himself in one swift move.

Reagan leaned her head back and laughed as his hands shook. Her hazel eyes turned a dark golden-green with burning passion, as vivid as her riot of auburn curls.

The air around them grew hot and savage. Kody reached for her as she had done to him, but with a shake of her head, Reagan pushed him flat on his back on the bed. Straddling his waist, she glared at him, daring him to deny her in any way.

"You made me wait," she gasped. "Now you wait…if you can."

And in that one instant, Kody found his heart. He refused to completely acknowledge it, of course, but deep inside, in a place where notions are formed and desires and fears are kept hidden, he recognized in her something that had been missing in himself.

Biting down on the inside of his cheek to stall the inevitable, he watched while this woman, who had all of a sudden become the woman in his dreams, pleased herself.

She was savage and tender at the same time, just the way he had been with her. Scraping his nipple lightly with her teeth, she drove him wild in the mirror image of his actions. Her short nails dug into his arms as she frantically touched every bit of him within her reach.

He surprised himself by moaning and writhing under

her. And when at last she lifted her hips and fitted herself down around his shaft, the pleasure of being inside her again was so great he nearly blacked out.

But he didn't want to miss an instant of this wondrous coupling. Reagan set the pace. She pulled up, then slid down. At one point, she growled from so low and deep in her gut he worried she might be injured. But not so.

Her eyes were glassy with desire, though he knew she had complete control of herself and the situation. Reaching behind their joined bodies, she gently cupped him.

This time, he arched his hips up off the bed and shouted, "No fair. I…can't…"

Laughing again, she lifted her hips and jammed her body down against his groin with such gentle force that he felt himself going to the greatest of her depths. Deeper than he'd thought possible.

Reagan screamed with pure pleasure. Her eyes widened and the look in them became feral, savage, unrestrained. Her expression was darkest fire. But underneath that was trust. Trust in him to let her be her.

It was that one look that really did it for him. He grabbed her hips and held her steady as he pounded into her at a pace that left them both breathless. In a momentary haze, Kody couldn't tell where his body ended and hers began.

He wanted to watch her come apart. To go with her to a special place neither of them had entered before. So he slowed the pace again and concentrated on the pleasure.

He'd been humbled by her, and more than a little shaken by what he saw in her eyes. She was giving him more of herself than she'd ever given to anyone. He'd be willing to stake his life on it.

Awed, he forced himself to give her more time by biting his lip. He really didn't deserve her.

You cannot have what you most desire, he chastised himself. Having her, holding her forever could, should and would never happen. It wasn't right for either of them.

Impatient with the slower pace, Reagan bent over and covered his mouth with her own. She went wild biting, soothing, sucking, licking.

"Now," she demanded against his lips.

And when she at last arched upward again, she had the most beautiful and determined smile on her face.

He would've given her anything.

Rolling his hips one final time, he felt the zing of ultimate pleasure surging through every cell in his body. All of a sudden he had to be the one who trusted—trusted her to come with him.

Pulsing, pouring his need into her, he discovered by some miracle that his soul had been found. When he hadn't even realized it had been lost.

Reagan's body began its internal convulsing, and she cried out her own release. He'd known all along she would be there with him when the time came. And here she was.

The two of them simply let the rest of the world fade away, while the light and knowledge surrounded, and then completed them.

Hours later, as the gray ghosts of dawn peeked around the bedroom curtains, Kody awoke to find rusty curls splayed across his chest and Reagan's even breathing tickling his neck. He didn't want to wake her. They hadn't managed much actual sleep during the sometimes wild night.

But he couldn't resist touching one of those plush curls. Wrapping the strands gently around his finger, Kody lay quietly and listened to their hearts beating in rhythm.

He couldn't quite get his mind around what was happening between them, or maybe it was just to him. Their night had been more than anything in his experience—or in his imagination. Erotic and primal. Easy and intense.

Rubbing Reagan's back in a gentle, soothing motion, Kody tried to sort out what she meant to him. Such internal musings were not the norm for a man who would rather take action than consider consequences.

It was time to consider what the future could possibly be for them, however.

He knew he would die for her. That was a given. If she wanted to find her father, Kody would search to the ends of the earth. If she wanted to stay in this bed and have him feed her between kisses, he would do it in a heartbeat.

But what if she wanted him to leave the reservation and go away with her forever? His heart flipped and squeezed at the thought. He'd given the Brotherhood his promise, and they had given him the secrets to fighting off the Skinwalkers in return.

Ever since his failed marriage to an Anglo who had insisted that they remain in the big city, he'd vowed never again to get involved with anyone. He had loved his ex-wife. Well, he thought he'd loved her. And it had hurt when he had been tossed aside like some half-breed boy toy.

Becoming a member of the Brotherhood and returning to his roots and his family had felt so right after all that pain. He'd been so sure that coming home would make him feel like part of the group, at last.

In truth, Dinetah still felt like the place where he must be in order to survive. The nightmares over his father's death had almost subsided when he'd first come back home and become a part of the Brotherhood. And they'd disappeared entirely the minute he began battling the Skinwalkers.

Kody believed he was born to be a man of the law, like his father before him. Finding the bad guys and bringing them to justice with the FBI was not exactly like being a master of disguise with the CIA, as his father had been before he retired.

But whether with the FBI, the Brotherhood or anywhere else, fighting for the good was what kept Kody going. Could he possibly consider giving it all up for her?

"What in the name of hell were you thinking?" Reagan sat straight up in bed and glared at him.

"Morning, Red."

"Don't 'morning' me, Agent Long." Reagan was fighting a pitched internal battle, trying desperately to get over the panic of finding herself naked in bed with a man she barely knew.

It was too easy to take out her regrets on the man instead of on herself. A flash of inspiration went through her head, reminding her that she would never in a million years regret one second she'd spent with Kody Long. But she shoved the idea aside.

No time for weaknesses now. Not when the fear of losing her control and her soul to a man who might not even give a damn was so strong it threatened to knock her over.

"You okay?"

Just his voice irritated her. "You…you…" Words nearly failed her. "You made me into something I'm not. I don't want to be the kind of woman who's that aggressive, that forward with men, that…"

"That sexy and spectacular?" He didn't even question her angry tone, but just lay there on his back, smiling up at her.

She inched away and slid off the side of the bed. "I'm going to take a shower."

Picking up her sweats from where they'd been pitched the night before, she refused to look at him. His face would haunt her dreams for the rest of her life. She'd blown it forever. No one else would ever be as gentle or as savage. She would never find another man like him. Never.

Oh yeah. The rest of her life would be full of regrets, all right. But it wouldn't be because of what she'd done with Kody. It would be because of what she'd tasted and lost.

"You want me to come help you in there?" he asked with a chuckle. "I'm a genius when it comes to washing backs."

"No," she said, more forcefully than she would've liked. "No, thanks. I'm good. But I'm starving…for food…. I'll just be a few minutes."

"Okay. I'll meet you in the kitchen."

She didn't want to think of meeting him again anywhere, so she ducked into the bathroom, slamming the door behind her. The memories of what they'd done during the night were seizing her heart with subtle hooks.

Reagan couldn't avoid or stop the images of his hands on her body. Or put an end to the pictures in her head of his mouth touching and especially tasting her into a wild frenzy. The thoughts of how she had behaved both excited and shamed her.

The whole thing had been such a paradigm shift in her ordered existence that she couldn't quite catch her breath. Hiding under the hot water and forcing her mind to go blank by her own will, she refused to consider the what-ifs.

Dammit. He'd made her breakfast.

A whole half an hour later, and she was still kicking herself for the loss of control last night.

But how could you hate a guy who was able to drive you crazy with one touch, and who also managed to cook a decent meal?

This was nuts. She was madly, desperately in love with Kody Long. And clearly, it was all wrong.

The way the two of them mixed was like a complicated formula in quantitative analysis that was nearly impossible to solve.

They could never have any kind of a future. Kody belonged here. It was as plain to her as prime numbers. He had roots and family. People who cared about him.

And she belonged…exactly nowhere.

Well, maybe she belonged with her Internet buddies online. But that was *so* nowhere. It was not as if any of *them* belonged in a real place. The guys on all her loops had addresses like "In-10-se," "4Pla" or "Super-Cyber-Guy." They were geeky outcasts like her.

She looked over at Kody, who was silently finishing his coffee, and felt warmth move along her arteries from her gut to her heart. He was so very real. So virile and exciting, yet comfortable and friendly.

Damn him, anyway.

Never before had she even so much as met a man who turned her on this way, let alone a guy who she wanted to spend the rest of her life with. She'd thought she liked having men as friends—distant friends.

And her online friendships were certainly a lot better than the guys she'd gone out with who'd wanted to hook up with her physically. Ugh. But there was no "ugh" factor where Kody was concerned.

Just the opposite, in fact. Crap. Wouldn't you know it? A guy who was totally wrong for her.

The ringing of the cell phone pinned to Kody's belt

broke the silence in the kitchen. He answered, threw her a dark look and stepped outside as if he didn't want her to hear his side of the conversation.

Well, that was fine. There were some things going on around this reservation that she didn't care to know about.

But then it hit her that the conversation might be about her father, and she changed her mind. Heading for the door, she met him coming back inside.

"Was that about my dad?"

"Not really, Red. But I'm needed. I have to go."

"What do you mean by 'not really'? And you sound like you expect to go without me. No way that's happening."

"Reagan," he began in a most patient tone of voice. "Sit down a minute."

His touch was more than gentle when he guided her back into the kitchen chair. But his eyes were saying something entirely different. The look in them said he would rather be touching her the way he had last night.

And that same expression also said it wasn't going to happen.

"Look. I..." Instead of joining her at the table, he turned and paced the kitchen floor. "Remember the discussion you had with Lucas at the café? The one about the silver bracelets and the Navajo men who wore them?"

She nodded. But he didn't seem to be paying much attention at the moment.

He glanced over at her, then quickly looked away. "A number of Navajo men, me included, have formed a special group in order to protect and serve the Dine. Sort of like an adjunct to the tribal police, who are always overwhelmed with work."

"That's cool. It sounds like a great volunteer job. Like being a volunteer fireman or something."

"Um, yeah. Like that. And they need me to serve with them this morning."

"Okay. I understand. But I thought you weren't supposed to leave me alone?"

He paced to her side and hesitated before he gently reached over and stroked her cheek. It was such a reverent gesture, so full of tenderness and silent longing, that she found herself battling sudden tears.

"You need to be safe. Roaming the countryside has not proved to be a terribly secure thing for you to do. The ones who took your numbers away…" He shook his head and turned to stare out the window. "You don't want to meet them in person. I can't worry about your safety and be a competent member of the Brotherhood at the same time."

"The Brotherhood?"

He turned back to her with a smile. "It's a cool name for a Navajo group dedicated to helping their clans and families on the reservation, don't you think?"

"Yeah. I like it a lot."

"Then you'll stay here, hidden and safe, while I go? It'll only be for a few hours. I'll have my mother's neighbor come here to stay with you. She's special. You can depend on her."

The thought of being without him, even for just a few hours, hurt. However, she figured she had better get used to the pain. She didn't belong on the reservation. And when her father was located and they were a family again, she would be going back to her old way of life—away from Navajoland…and away from Kody.

"Okay," she said, trying to hide her anguish. "I'll stay."

Chapter 13

*B*lood everywhere.

Kody's first impression of the scene shocked and horrified him. The SUV's burned out interior did not disguise the bloody evidence of murder. Kody cringed and his stomach rolled as the metallic scent of dried blood assaulted his senses.

A man's body lay up against a dry, dusty boulder, his limbs twisted into unnatural positions. He was obviously dead. His face and head of thick black hair appeared to be pretty much intact, which seemed odd, considering that his neck and upper chest had been ripped to shreds by some unknown, savage entity. Still, the victim should be easy enough to identify.

"What do think happened here?" he asked his brother.

Hunter Long scanned the sandstone cliffs above them. "This was a Skinwalker attack. But we have only one victim, and more blood than could've come from a single man. We don't have any motive. And there were no telltale vibrations beforehand."

"Then why are you so sure the attackers were the evil ones?"

Hunter answered by pointing to the ground near the passenger door. "Check it out."

Kody slid a quick glance toward the print in the clay under the car. "A coyote?" He squatted to inspect the damp impression, half-hidden under the SUV.

"No," he said, contradicting himself. "A wolf." Spreading his fingers along the ridges, Kody tried to judge the size of the animal who'd left the huge track.

"The Navajo Wolf," Hunter agreed. "The wolf of legends. And quite likely also a real-life modern man who heads our enemy band of Skinwalkers."

Hunkering down beside him, Hunter continued, "The vic's death appears to have been caused by a wild animal attack, but it looks almost surgically clean. We'll have to wait for a final judgment.

"And, bro," Hunter added with a glance around, "there's also evidence of a large snake who accompanied the wolf."

"A snake?" Well, damn. Kody had seen a large snake recently. And he'd seen it less than a half mile from here, in the newly discovered ruin at Backwash Monument.

That first night when Reagan had lost the numbers.

The two brothers stood, but kept their voices low. "You think a Skinwalker has found the secret of turning himself into a snake? That's not one of the animal forms that legends describe."

Hunter shrugged, but eyed the rocky surfaces nearby where a snake might be concealed. "There have long been stories of such shape-shifting, but most people chalked them up to drunken rumors. I believe these modern Skin-walkers have turned the legends upside down. All things are possible."

Hunter continued when he seemed sure Kody had gotten his meaning. "Our Brotherhood cousin from the Red Lake area, Michael Ayze, the high school teacher and part-time anthropologist, is tracking the signs right now.

"He's farther up in this canyon. And predictably, he just called to say they all lead in the direction of your newly discovered ruin."

Hunter hesitated again, but after a moment's consideration, he added, "It's not for certain, but in my opinion, the depth of the wolf's tracks indicates that something…or someone…was carried away from here."

"You believe another person was in the SUV and the Skinwalkers have taken him away?"

Hunter nodded.

Kody understood what his brother was really saying. Hunter was the best tracker Kody knew about. That included uniquely trained U.S. Special Forces and so-called expert Native American trackers who claimed to be world class.

Was it possible that this apparent kidnapping was evidence that Reagan's father had really been captured by Skinwalkers? Though he hadn't said it in so many words, Hunter believed someone important had been spirited away from this bloody scene.

Kody turned his head, looking off to the northwest, in the direction of the secret side canyon and ruin he and Reagan had discovered. The dry, chilly winter wind slapped him in the face as it zinged down the narrowing, red-rock arroyo where he stood.

"I will contact Michael by cell phone, Perhaps he could use your help with his search," Hunter stated.

"Will you also be notifying the FBI about the murder?"

"In time," Hunter replied. The corners of his lips twitched. "You're on leave and this location is hours away from any FBI field office or tribal subagency office. Maybe I'll collect more evidence first and then call my tribal police captain so he can notify the feds of the unnatural death."

"The one who has been killed," Kody began, observing the traditional Navajo taboo of not speaking directly about the dead. "Doesn't appear to be a member of the Dine." He glanced in the direction of the body, then quickly looked away.

"I agree. Looks more Greek or Italian…maybe Middle Eastern…to me." Hunter tilted his head in the subtle manner of the Navajo. "Doesn't seem like there will be a need for anyone to put this body into the ground by nightfall. No clan will be nearby to claim it."

Kody nodded. "In addition to the lack of religious and traditional reasons, I'd imagine the FBI will be ordering an autopsy of the dead man. There's no compelling need for you to rush your investigation.

"However, keep in mind that someone may have been abducted from here and may be in mortal danger."

Without responding, Hunter flipped open his cell phone and called Michael Ayze. In less than a moment, Michael agreed to meet Kody at a halfway point.

As he prepared to walk up the rocky wash to the meeting place, Hunter stopped him with a hand to the shoulder. "Where is the *bilagáana* woman whose father may be missing?" he asked. "Has she returned to her home in California?"

"She's staying at our mother's house for the time being," Kody replied. "Just until we can get a line on her father's whereabouts."

"Was it wise to leave her?"

Hunter's lack of an agreeable response clearly showed what he thought about leaving a defenseless woman at the mercy of the Skinwalkers.

An hour later, after Kody and Michael had met up and then split again in order to cover a wider search area, Kody was still thinking back to his brother's disapproving expression during their last conversation.

As he climbed an aluminum ladder, heading toward a cliff ruin in the Backwash area, he began to chastise himself for leaving her. He hadn't really liked the idea at the time, but he had strongly felt his responsibility to the Brotherhood.

Swallowing back the choking worry, he kept reminding himself that Shirley Nez should be there. And as his mentor and teacher, she would never let anything bad happen to Reagan. He was positive.

Reagan finished the dishes and went in search of the wireless handheld device that she hoped was fully charged by now. She needed information and was also dying to contact a couple of her computer buddies. It had been days since she'd been online and she worried that her mailbox would be jammed with out-of-date messages and spam that had managed to get through all her filters.

She found the jacket on the floor in her temporary bedroom. Man, she sure hoped she would be able to get a good cell phone connection here in the wilderness. She knew there wouldn't be any Wi-Fi nearby.

Though she loved the cozy atmosphere of Mrs. Long's house, her whole tradition-based life was just a little too retro to make Reagan feel at home.

Jamming a hand into her jacket pocket to find the Blackberry, Regan stopped when she suddenly heard a soft knocking. It seemed to be coming from the kitchen door. Imagining that it was the neighbor Kody had said would be visiting, Reagan threw the jacket back on the bed with the phone still in the pocket and went to let the woman in.

Right before she put out her hand to turn the door-knob, it occurred to Reagan that she had better check to see who was really knocking. Standing on tiptoes, she peeked through the decorative windows at the top of the door. Being five-nine was good for a few things, after all.

On the other side of the door and slightly below her line of sight, an older woman stood waiting to be let in. The Native American lady wore a shabby but colorful scarf covering her gray hair, and a long-sleeved shirt in a deep purple color.

Though not able to get a good look at the woman's face, Reagan did see that she was carrying what seemed to be a covered cake plate. The old lady must indeed be Kody's neighbor. Who else would come bearing gifts?

But her build seemed a bit thicker than the other women Reagan had met up to now on the reservation. Still, this old person could not be a threat to anyone.

Opening the door, Reagan found herself staring at sad eyes and an even sadder pair of rubber boots underneath an ankle-length skirt that seemed to contain every color known to man. The person introduced herself as Shirley, and in a minute or two, Reagan felt comfortable enough to let her come inside.

Once she was across the threshold, the woman's appearance changed. She suddenly didn't look quite so old. Instead of stooped, she stood tall and erect, almost the same height as Reagan. Her eyes, a depthless black, darted purposefully in every direction. She was studying the room in what seemed like a boarding school inspection.

"I baked a cake," the old lady said as she shoved the plate at Reagan. "Special clan recipe."

"Um, thank you." Reagan set the plate on the kitchen counter and removed the cover. "It looks delicious."

The cake smelled good, but it was plastered with a frosting that resembled coconut. Not Reagan's favorite.

"I will make coffee," the neighbor murmured. "We will sit. Talk. Eat. The time will go fast."

"Uh, okay." Reagan sat down at the kitchen table and watched as she rummaged around in the cabinets, looking for the proper things to make coffee.

An odd thought flashed through Reagan's mind—the idea that this scene was somehow all wrong. But the spark of inspiration was a high-speed notion, moving in and out of her consciousness like a bullet, so she shrugged it off.

"Have you known Kody Long for a long time?" Shirley asked as she continued working at the kitchen counter.

"Only for a few days." Another something nudged at Reagan's awareness, but whatever it was stayed buried in the recesses of her brain.

"His past is full of regrets," the older woman said in a deep, serious tone. "There is talk that he could have saved his father's life, but did nothing because of his half-breed fears."

Reagan started to interrupt with questions, but decided to stay quiet instead. Her thoughts had already turned to the man she loved, whom she wanted to come home more than anything else on earth.

As if an unseen light switch had been suddenly thrown, savage, erotic images descended upon Reagan and began to consume her, body and mind.

"He was treated horribly by that wicked city woman he

married, too," Shirley continued blithely. "But I'm not sure what he could've expected from such a mixed marriage. A *bilagáana* woman is not to be trusted…."

The old lady stopped and turned to give Reagan a hesitant smile. "Sorry. No offense?"

Reagan shook her head and blinked back most of the wild images in her head. But now she felt positive that something was quite wrong here.

She barely managed to stand up. As she looked directly into the elder's eyes, her knees became wobbly and her head began to hurt.

Instead of the eyes she had expected to see, Reagan saw something she was forced to classify as pure evil. Watery images blurred her vision as the face of an ugly, middle-aged man with acne-scarred skin and sharp fang teeth took the place of the old woman. Reagan had to grab hold of the kitchen table with both hands in an effort to stay steady.

"May I help you?" she managed to ask in a hoarse voice.

The woman had swung around and was pouring cold water into the pot with her back to Reagan. "No, thank you. I…" She stopped in midsentence and stared out the window over the sink.

It felt as if hours passed before the woman shut off the faucet and spoke again. "I'm sorry. I've forgotten an important appointment. I must go now."

"Oh?"

The old lady turned, wiped her hands on her skirt and narrowed her eyes at Reagan. "I must go. Don't forget to eat a piece of that cake. I made it just for you."

"Well, if you must…." Reagan waved toward the door, and the woman disappeared through it so fast it seemed like a blurred fast-forward on an old-fashioned VCR.

Reagan collapsed at the table and dropped her head in her hands. Whew! Something had really gotten to her.

Resting for a moment and trying to sort through her impressions, she soon realized that getting her thoughts back in order was turning out to be a lot harder than she had imagined. Earlier, she had noticed an effort someone was making to control her mind from afar. But what had just gone on around her, here in Audrey Long's home?

Reagan got up on unsteady feet in order to check out the back door window again, wondering why she hadn't heard the old lady's car driving away. Shirley had been just plain scary, and now Reagan's mind was filling with all kinds of questions about the weird neighbor.

Had that creaky woman walked over here? And had she intended to walk home when, according to Kody, she lived more than a quarter mile away? Reagan stretched on tiptoes again and her breath caught in her throat. She couldn't see the woman in any direction she checked.

Had the neighbor just disappeared? Hairs on the back of Reagan's neck stood straight up on end and goose bumps covered her arms. But then an ancient two-door car with rusted fenders and a cracked rear window drove into the yard and stopped. Reagan's whole body began to tremble.

It didn't take her more than two seconds to run to the bedroom and grab the Blackberry. She got a faint signal, but it was enough to make her call.

She had memorized Kody's cell number. Punching it in, she raced back toward the kitchen door while waiting for him to answer.

He was on the line in one ring. "Yes?"

"Kody, it's me. Tell me what your neighbor, Shirley, looks like."

"What? Why…"

She peeked out the window again and saw something that cleared her mind immediately. The explanation for everything that had felt wrong seemed to jab her right between the eyes.

Outside, standing next to the beat-up car, was a well-dressed, middle-aged woman waiting patiently for someone to invite her inside.

"How stupid could I be?" Reagan groaned with pure self-disgust, slapping her forehead with her palm.

"What's wrong, Red? Do you need me?" Kody's voice was filled with concern.

"I'll just bet your mother's neighbor…what was her name? Shirley Nez, right? Well, I'll bet she owns a seventies era, green, two-door sedan, doesn't she?"

"Yes, she does, but—"

"Never mind." Reagan groaned again. She had no intention of scaring him or causing him any more worry than necessary. "Go on with what you were doing. I'm perfectly fine. The neighbor is here and everything will be terrific after I let her inside."

"If you're sure you're okay…" Kody mumbled hesitantly, as if he didn't know whether to panic or not.

"I'm positive. Bye."

Reagan ended the call and unlocked the door. Stepping out on the porch to beckon the neighbor inside, she ticked off in her brain all the incredibly stupid things that she'd missed over the last half hour while she had visited with a very strange—and possibly very dangerous—old lady.

No traditional Navajo would ever be unthinking enough to approach someone's door without first being invited inside. Ben's words came back to remind her of her first dumb move.

Navajos try never to be rude to anyone, Kody had said. Reagan suspected that rummaging around in someone's cupboards without being asked would probably be classified as quite rude.

Traditional Navajos never use given names when talking to or about other Navajos. Reagan had totally forgotten Lucas's caution. How could she? Really dumb.

She waved at the real neighbor, who smiled and came toward her. By the time Shirley Nez was inside the kitchen, Reagan's words were spilling out of her mouth like water over a dam.

"And the old witch brought that funny-looking cake on the counter over there and insisted I eat a bite." She heard herself gushing, while showing Shirley into the kitchen. "And she said stuff about Kody's past that made me wonder if she wasn't trying to drive doubts about him into my mind…and…"

Shirley Nez's smile turned to a scowl. "Take a breath. Calm down. Tell me—"

"And when I stopped paying real close attention to what she was saying," Reagan blurted, as if she'd never been interrupted, "my mind started to go blank and the numbers began to disappear again…and—"

Kody's neighbor turned without a word, picked up the cake plate and put the whole thing into the garbage can. It was such a rash move that Reagan stopped talking.

"Sit down and catch your breath," Shirley ordered. "I have to make a quick call and then we'll get rid of this evil potion. We can burn it before Lucas arrives. He'll be coming to hold a short Sing for you. I wish we had the time to do more, but unfortunately, the longer ceremony will have to wait."

Once again Reagan collapsed into the chair, stunned by

the images Shirley's words had conjured. But right away her mind began churning with new thoughts and questions.

"Uh, please excuse me, Kody's neighbor and mentor," she began, addressing the other woman tentatively, as she remembered Lucas teaching her. "But can you tell me about the Brotherhood?"

Shirley stopped with the phone halfway to her ear. She turned and silently studied Reagan's face.

"And while you're at it," Reagan continued in a brand-new and surprisingly forceful voice, "I want to know the whole truth. Every single thing you can tell me about the evil ones. And all you ever knew about Skinwalkers."

Chapter 14

Kody blinked back a shaft of fear, closing his eyes to the panic as he looked down at two hundred feet of nothing but air between himself and solid ground. It was so quiet he imagined hearing the drops of his sweat hitting the sand below.

Just where was the Brotherhood and all his clan when he really needed them? Digging his fingers farther into sandstone crevices, he nearly laughed at his own stupidity. How could anyone with half a brain, who knew what he was facing, turn their backs on a Skinwalker?

Good question. Maybe he would review his bad actions if he lived through the consequences.

The first thing that Shirley had instilled in them was to never turn your back on the enemy unless another Brotherhood member was right there to watch that back. He'd also supposedly learned that same lesson long ago at Quantico.

So he guessed that made him a double loser.

His cell phone began to vibrate in his shirt pocket. Wedging the toes of his rubber soled moccasins ever deeper into tiny cracks in the face of the sheer cliff, he ignored the call.

If that was Reagan again, calling to tell him something horrible had happened to her because he'd made the mistake of leaving her alone, he couldn't face it. Not that he had a free hand at the moment, anyway.

Guessing that he should probably say a few prayers, he began with one of the ancient chants. Kody figured he might as well try to do away with that rat of a Skinwalker snake by saying the right chant—*if* he could manage to get it all out of his mouth before he fell to his death.

He'd been *so* not smart. Maybe he deserved to die. He had not followed Brotherhood prescribed commandments, and hadn't even called Michael when he'd clearly spotted the snake's trail and continued to track it alone.

Less than an hour ago Michael had been right beside him, cautioning that if they were going to split up and take different trails, the first one to see any sign of the evil ones must contact the other before he continued on. The operative word in that sentence had obviously been *before*. Too late now.

Right then, Kody heard the sound of flapping wings directly above him as they cut through the air unseen. They seemed to be big wings—really big wings. As Red might've said, *Ah, crap.*

All Kody could do was hang on and hope like hell it wasn't a vulture. He was definitely *not* ready to give up just yet.

"You need a hand, brother?" The sound of Hunter's voice calling down from the clifftop above him might as well have been angels singing.

Kody could only manage a grunt. But if his brother didn't stop asking stupid questions and get on with saving his life, Kody would probably be hearing the sound of angels for real—and soon.

As he grabbed the rope Hunter threw down to him, he started shouting orders, realizing he wasn't about to die. Cursing all the way up the side of the cliff, he scrambled over the edge and into his brother's waiting arms.

"You have quite a vivid Anglo vocabulary, cousin." Michael Ayze stood smiling at him from right behind Hunter's back.

Kody fell facedown on the flat stone of the cleft in the cliff where they stood, and nearly kissed the ground. "You haven't heard anything yet," he told his cousin with gritted teeth. He lay on his belly, trying to catch his breath.

When he'd finally gulped in enough air to speak without gasping, Kody decided he needed answers from the two Brotherhood members who had saved his life. "How'd you know I was in trouble? And how on earth did you find me?"

Hunter studied him for a moment. "You weren't answering your cell. And it didn't automatically go to voice mail. That meant you must be having problems."

"Hmm."

"The Bird People were the ones who found you," Michael added. "Our cousin Lucas Tso learned of the trouble and asked them for assistance."

"How did you end up over the side of the cliff?" Hunter asked. "Did the evil ones hit you with a surprise attack?"

Kody found his balance at last and stood up on still-shaky legs. "Don't ask," he muttered, not yet willing to admit his own stupidity. "But I did look directly into the face of the Skinwalker snake. And I felt a strong craving in him for Reagan. I have to get back to her.

"That whole contrived kidnapping scene back at the mouth of the canyon…" he added in a stronger, more confident voice. "The car, the wolf tracks, everything was just a distraction for us. I'm positive someone designed it just to throw us off."

"Yes," Michael agreed. "It certainly threw you right off the side of the cliff."

Kody knew he should smile at his cousin's subtle, Navajo-style humor. But he was too concerned about Reagan to do much of anything but rush back to her.

Dusting himself off, Kody felt his growing anxiety over Reagan's safety creating a lump in his throat. But he wasn't quite ready to phone her just yet. Not without knowing if a real person had been abducted from the bloody and burned out SUV. And if that person could've been her father.

Instead, he would have Hunter call Shirley to check on Reagan. Kody needed to hear that she was still safe and sound so his life could get back on track.

Looking mortality and pure evil in the eye tended to change a man. But since his brain was still misted over by a fog of panic and guilt, he wouldn't be able to judge how much he'd changed for quite a while yet.

All he knew now was that he, too, craved Reagan, just like the snake. And that craving was growing stronger and deeper with every breath he took.

Reagan paced the wood-planked kitchen floor, waiting for Kody to return to his mother's house. She'd heard what had happened to him and couldn't wait to see him.

Shirley and Lucas were outside, circling the house and using chants and sacred medicines to bless and return it to balance and safety. Clasping and unclasping her hands, and occasionally stopping to bite her nails, Reagan tried to force her thoughts away from Kody and on to another subject entirely.

She'd done what she could with e-mail and text messages on her handheld wireless, but an old-fashioned, reliable computer was what she needed most.

Kody must know the whereabouts of a computer that she could use to dial into the Internet. Shirley had been hinting that the Brotherhood used such a computer for research.

Reagan had her own research to do.

Even without a computer, she had learned a lot in the last few hours from Shirley and then from Lucas about the Skinwalkers and the Brotherhood. Their stories had been fascinating. The chants, rituals and medicines they used were complicated, but mostly based on things Reagan had already heard or read about.

When they'd first told her about the Skinwalkers, Reagan had wondered if the entire reservation wasn't suffering from some form of mass hypnosis. But in the end, she had no choice except to believe the truth.

Her own empirical evidence was impossible to ignore. She had experienced it in person.

She'd seen and heard almost everything she needed to find her father. But she was still expecting helpful information to come in via e-mail. And she couldn't wait to get her hands on it.

She'd text messaged one of her online buddies, who had promised to hack into an underground database in order to get the information she'd requested. A competent and notorious cracker, this friend wouldn't take more than a few hours to find what she needed.

Reagan hoped getting hold of this particular information would not mean the destruction of her childhood dreams. She had focused everything about who and what she had become on girlish imaginings of a father she scarcely knew. Now she would finally learn the truth.

She just had to pray Kody would never find out how she had gotten the information.

"Red? You okay?" Speak of the devil.

She turned around to see Kody coming into the kitchen through the mudroom door. And it happened again. The sight of him was so stunning and so…familiar that she almost lost her mind.

In fact, she did lose control. Reagan held her breath and ran straight for him. "Ohmigod!" she shrieked. "You're here and you're…you're alive!"

It would have been embarrassing and truly terrible if Kody hadn't held out his arms and wrapped her up in his embrace as she came within reach. But he did.

Oh, glory, but he did.

He crushed her to his chest and held on tight, just as though he was still back there grasping the edge of that cliff. He'd thought he must be over any lingering adrenaline rush by this time. But when he felt her heart thumping wildly against his own, the blood rushed through his veins and he had to beat back blurry tears.

He never cried. Not even when his father died.

And now would not be the best time to begin. But Reagan felt so right in his arms. Her clean, fresh scent teased his senses. Her silky red curls tickled his neck.

The stoic inside him had given way to a man who'd been terrified that she might not be here when he returned.

Her rounded curves were plastered against him, making his thoughts turn to wild imaginings. He was a fool to want her this much. A fool and a romantic idiot.

She was in danger, and it was up to him to keep her safe.

He tried once again to remember his vows not to get involved with any woman.

He also remembered that his track record was not good when it came to picking the right person to love.

So he took her by the shoulders and gently set her back a few inches. "Uh…" Her face was so full of desire and caring that he forgot what he'd wanted to say.

"They told me," she began with a watery sniff. "You…you almost died. The Skinwalker snake pushed you off a cliff. I—I…"

Kody could see her battling tears the same way he had just been doing. The sight was endearing. It made him feel closer to her. As strong-willed and full of power as he knew she was, it seemed her heart was also in proper balance.

"Well, that's almost the way it happened." He managed a small smile. "And apparently *you* had a visitor who brought poison cake. You think maybe we should stick together from now on, or at least until we get a lead on your father?"

She didn't answer, but continued to gaze up at him with such longing that he couldn't bear to look at her beautiful face or the desire in those wide, hazel eyes for another second.

He turned to the sink and poured himself a glass of water. "I could use a shower. I'll get cleaned up while you—"

"Wait a second. Do you have any idea why these… these subhumans behave like this? What drives them?"

Swallowing the long, cool drink, Kody let the life-giving liquid calm him and settle his libido before he answered her question. "Navajo legend says the Skinwalkers are driven to do bad deeds in their thirst for power. Today that means money and all the things it can buy. Greed, pure and simple."

He turned around and saw the confusion in Reagan's eyes.

"But my ancestors amassed great wealth and power," she insisted. "And though they weren't exactly angels, not a single one of them went that far over to the dark side."

"Some people are just plain evil, Red. Maybe it's the way they were brought up—maybe it's destiny. Whatever causes it," he continued, "the good forces must battle the evil…and win. Otherwise, civilization as we know it will crumble."

Reagan placed her hand lightly on his arm. "This is personal for you, isn't it?"

Hell. He would rather cut out his tongue than rehash his old demons with her. But he wanted her to know what pure evil they were facing.

"The war means everything to me now." His answer had to explain why, otherwise he would not have told the whole truth. "But it began with my father's murder. The tribal police claimed at first that his death was a suicide."

Kody shook his head vehemently. "Our family knew better than that. Someone, or maybe some group, made it seem like Dad had turned from being a good cop to being a criminal. Like he'd been taking dirty money for giving out contracts. And that when he believed other investigators were closing in on him, he killed himself rather than face prison time."

"Your father was a cop, too?"

"At the time, he was a retired CIA agent, consulting with the Navajo tribal police on setting up a special investigations department."

The place on Kody's forearm where her hand still touched his skin grew warm. "But that's all ancient history. At first, I tried everything I could to prove his death was murder. But I wasn't sure what needed to be done. So I went off to college to study law enforcement, and then was recruited by the FBI."

"That's good. Maybe now you can find out what happened."

Gently tugging his arm away from her fingers, Kody shook his head. "That trail is too old. The clues are cold. But unfortunately, the same evil is spreading.

"There's a good chance that the Skinwalkers are looking to take over more than just this reservation." He backed up another step, because the urge to fold her in his embrace and protect her from the evil was so strong he could almost taste it. "The Brotherhood believes the bad guys won't stop until they have enough power to control the world."

Reagan's eyes widened and he could see her genius mind racing to put the pieces together. "I need—"

The kitchen door opened and Shirley Nez came inside. "The signs are growing darker."

She gave Kody a sharp nod, but concentrated her attention on Reagan. "You must use all your resources. Before it is beyond hope."

"Have you heard something about my father?"

"The winds are whispering many things tonight." Shirley turned to Kody. "You and your clan are being used…threatened. Not for deeds but for proximity."

"The Skinwalkers need Reagan." It was a pure guess, but he knew it to be the truth. "And they don't mind who they hurt or kill to get to her."

Shirley blinked once in response. "Your best defense is to stand behind the daughter. Give her whatever weapons she requires."

"Weapons?" He shifted to question Reagan. "What do you need? How can I help you?"

"A computer." The words slipped out of her mouth. "I

could really use a landline computer with Internet access if you've got one."

Why had she been so quick to ask for that? She chided herself that the last thing she needed right now was for Kody to ask why she wanted Internet access so desperately.

But he never missed a beat. "Come with me. I'll help you boot up and then I can grab a shower."

More than an hour later, Kody finally managed to slip into clean jeans, jam his feet into moccasins and comb his fingers through his still-wet hair. It hadn't taken five minutes to turn over the computer in his own hogan to Reagan. She'd had no trouble getting online.

But since then, his ear had been glued to his cell phone. Half a dozen Brotherhood members had called or been called. Kody wanted everyone to be on the lookout for trouble—and to search for a spot where the Skinwalkers might be holding Reagan's father captive.

This whole thing had something to do with Commander Wilson's classified job at White Sands. Kody was sure of it. Maybe he should try calling in a few of the favors he was owed in Washington to find out what Reagan's scientist father had been working on when he disappeared. Knowing that might tell them why.

Kody folded his towel and hung it on the rack. He'd deliberately built this round, wooden-planked building to be big enough for only one person.

It was the exact dimensions specified by tradition for a hogan. But he'd secretly run electric, telephone and cable TV up here so he and the Brotherhood could keep up with the bad guys.

He wondered how long Reagan would be staying with

him. Would she want to use the shower? What about sleeping arrangements?

Whoa. That was a thought he needed to bank. There would be no sleeping together. None. It would be too tempting.

And he just knew that the moment her father was found, Reagan would be gone. Back to her own life in California.

He was sure that would be for the best. If he went against his vows and asked her to stay, she might feel obligated—for a while.

But then, eventually, she would grow tired of him, tired of reservation life, and leave. Caring about Reagan and watching her walk away would be so much worse than when Marsha had left. It would kill him for sure this time.

Worrying about what Reagan had been up to since he'd last seen her, Kody wandered out of the bathroom and through the tiny kitchen toward the big central room under the domed roof. The closer he came, the more he could hear music playing. Hot music. Something with a salsa beat.

He spotted Reagan through the flickering shadows. She was on her feet and swaying her hips to the pounding beat.

Hanging back a second, he tried to see what she was up to. She was using the computer to play music from some Internet Web site. But that wasn't the most interesting part of what she was doing.

She had obviously discovered where he'd stored his mother's blank sketch pad. Kody had kept her old drawing paper, hoping that someday his mother would want to go back to her art. But so far, she had shown no interest.

Reagan, on the other hand, was using the pad to dash off something at a sprinter's pace. She was writing so fast it made him wonder why her wrist didn't ache.

As he watched, she finished filling the sheet she'd been

using, and ripped it off the pad. In two swift movements, she'd hung the sheet up on the hogan's log wall, fastening it with a piece of masking tape Kody had almost forgotten he owned.

He noticed it wasn't the first sheet she'd hung up that way. But instead of studying her handiwork, Reagan went right back to scribbling on the pad of paper.

Curious now, he drew closer for a better look. She was so wrapped up in what she was doing, he made it all the way to the wall where the papers were hanging and she never even noticed he was in the room.

"Math formulas?" He didn't mean to say the words out loud, but he was so struck with surprise that he couldn't contain himself.

"Huh?" Reagan looked up at him as though her mind had been a million miles away in some distant cosmos.

"What are you doing? What is all this?"

She shrugged a shoulder. "I saw the idea on a repeat of a television show. They got a few minor things wrong on TV, but I thought it might be worth a try." She looked over to where the papers were hanging. "I actually think it will work, too...or at least get us close."

"Can you give a poor math-impaired cop an idea of what you're talking about?"

She pointed to one paper that looked different from the rest. Moving closer for a better view, Kody noticed it was a computer-generated satellite map of the Four Corners reservation, with most of the roads overlaid on top.

"It's all in the numbers," she told him. "In this case, the idea is to find out *where* the Skinwalkers are located, not who they are. Human beings...even subhumans like Skin-walkers...will try to spread their bad deeds around an area in what appears to be a random pattern. They want to control the situation by hiding their true point of origin. Keeping their hideout a secret.

"But," she continued, pointing at several pages with formulas scribbled across them, "they never manage true random sequence. True random will include clusters. But this…" She waved at the wall of papers.

"What is *this?*"

"It's a mathematical principle for finding an origin point by working backward, using the scatter effect technique. It's similar to being able to find a black hole by using only the evidence of the effect that hole has on the galaxy around it."

"If you say so."

"Look." She tapped a finger on the map. "Here are all the locations where the Skinwalkers have attacked us. See? Backwash Monument. Sheepdip Creek. That cliff you tried climbing without a ladder."

He shook his head and smiled at her.

"But I'm missing something."

"What?"

"Well, since formulaic principle is never wrong, there should have been an attack—" she pointed to the map "—right in this area. But…"

"The Tuba City area?"

She nodded.

A chill moved up from the base of his spine and clutched at his heart. "There was an attack there. My mother's sister and her family."

"Ohmigod. That's where your mother went, isn't it?"

He didn't take the time to answer, but grabbed for his cell phone and headed out the door so he could get a better signal.

Before he had time to punch in his aunt's numbers, a

call came through. He looked at the lighted dial and his worst fears became reality. It was Shirley Nez calling. And Shirley was always the bearer of bad tidings.

He held his breath and answered her call.

Chapter 15

"Tell me again. Why are you and Shirley Nez so sure your mother's accident was a Skinwalker attack?"

Reagan sat hunched over the sketch pad in the passenger seat as Kody sped along through the gathering dusk. They were heading for a medical clinic in Window Rock, where Audrey Long had been admitted after being injured in a single vehicle rollover.

"And why was she way over near Window Rock? That's in the other direction from Tuba City." The questions and possible answers swirled in Reagan's head. She couldn't seem to help spitting them out as they occurred to her.

Kody threw her a wicked glance. "If you'll let me get in a word…"

She leaned back in the passenger seat and clamped her mouth shut.

He chuckled, but quickly sobered and returned his main

focus to the mountainous road ahead. "According to Shirley, my mother and her brother-in-law were returning to Tuba City after spending the day in Window Rock. They'd tried to see the tribal council about the massacre of the sheep, but didn't have much luck. The council is in session, but even my aunt and uncle's own chapter delegate refused to listen."

"Why?"

"A couple of reasons, probably. In the first place, there's a lot of political turmoil these days about loose dogs on the rez. The People have strong opinions about letting animals be animals in Navajoland and not trying to make them over into some white man's version of a pet."

Kody's gaze never seemed to waver from the road. Staying strictly in one lane, the truck wove in and out of the ever darkening shadows cast by the tall spires of peach-colored sandstone and the tips of mountains to the west.

"But you and your mother don't believe the sheep attack was done by wild dogs, do you?"

He shook his head. "Definitely Skinwalkers. But the politicians are even more reluctant to talk about them than they are about loose dogs.

"The car rolling over was no accident, either," he added. "The shadowed form of an animal they didn't recognize shot out in front of them on the highway. When my uncle swerved, he said the car careened out of control just as if it were sliding on glass."

"How awful," Reagan said with a shudder. "If the light was a little better, I could plug the GPS coordinates for your mother's accident into the formula. I'm sure it will be the last piece of information we need to complete the equation and narrow down the point of origin to perhaps a ten-mile radius."

"Sorry. Can't risk a light right now."

Reagan hugged the sketch pad to her chest. "You mean you're feeling it, too?"

He shrugged. "I've been getting the vibrations for the last fifteen minutes. What do you feel?"

"A presence. Someone watching." She shrugged as he had, then turned to look at him. "And a growing desperation to throw myself at you."

The laugh he barked was self-deprecating and rather sad. "We're not ever going to be able to get around that, are we, Red?"

She wasn't sure what to say to him. Their conversation had turned too intimate for someone of her limited experience.

Unable to think of the right words, she opened her mouth and said the first thing that came to her. "The sex we had the last time…the time when my head was clear…was fantastic. I wouldn't mind doing it over again."

Oh man. Those words were all wrong. The sketch pad dropped to her lap as she began flapping her hands and waggling her fingers with nervous energy.

"I—I mean," she stuttered, "we hardly know each other, and as soon as we find my father, I'll be leaving, going back home. I mean, do you think we should continue…"

Reagan gulped for air. "What I mean is, I'm not that kind of a person. I'm *not* someone who just jumps in the sack for a night or two. No matter how fabulous it was."

Kody reached over and captured her left hand, stilling the flying fingers and calming her nerves. "Easy, Red."

Reagan could see he was struggling for the right words, too. His jaw clenched and unclenched.

"I've spent the last eleven years of my life learning how to keep my emotions in check," he finally murmured as he laced his fingers with hers. "But then you ran into my life, both literally and figuratively, and changed everything.

"That wasn't fair of you," he added with an exhalation.

She heard the hurt and hesitation mixed together in his voice. It made her want to climb into his lap and wrap her arms around him, soothing whatever was bothering him.

Which was a really weird idea, since she had never done such a thing with anyone before in her entire life.

Despite wanting to help him, she could not come up with any words that would make a difference. What should she say to him?

Kody made it easier when he spoke first. "It's not just the sex, Red. It's you. Who you are. An intelligent and attractive woman with an inner strength of spirit that is more than just a sexual turn-on. It's…addictive."

She hiccupped a laugh. "Me? Be serious. Sure, I'm fairly smart. And I'm real good with guys, all right. But as buddies—friends." She shook her head so hard her neck ached. "I'm just not the type to interest men. When you come right down to it, I guess I'm also not so hot relating to women. Or to kids. Or even to pets."

Despite the dark shadow that currently covered his face, she knew Kody was smiling. "Yeah," he agreed. "You do put up a bunch of subconscious barriers to keep everyone away. But I've seen you when those doors were accidentally left open. People are drawn to you."

"People?"

"My cousins in the Brotherhood. My mother." He hesitated. "Me, especially."

Blinking her eyes, she tried her best to understand what he was trying to say. She did love him. But there could never be a future for them.

She did not belong here. And he did.

Just then, she felt the pull of someone else's will.

In the back of her mind, she'd been expecting it. But suddenly it was all she could do to defend herself against the attack. Tugging her hand free of Kody's, she pressed her fingers to her temples and concentrated.

"Reagan? What's wrong…."

She leaned back in the seat and shook her head. "Attack. Let me…let me think."

Kody shut his mouth and scowled. She was so strong and extraordinary. He was positive she could defend herself. But his frustration at not being able to help her nearly caused him to stop the truck in order to get out and fight off the evil with his bare hands.

But he knew he would only be fighting shadows. The real evil was harder to capture, harder to define.

He grabbed the steering wheel with a deadly grip and pressed his foot down on the gas. Concentrating on getting them away from the danger in one piece was his best plan. His only plan.

The Navajo Wolf pushed away from his dinner table and excused himself.

He was losing a measure of hard-won control. The hint in the air of the Snake's losing mind-battle with the Anglo woman had driven the Wolf to take leave from his guests.

Turning his back on Sheik Bashshar and his tuxedoed henchman at the dining table, the Wolf fought to maintain his human persona in the presence of the Snake's negative energy. The Wolf ran his tongue lightly over his front teeth, checking. The fangs were still concealed. Good enough for the time being. At least until he could get his hands on that idiot Snake.

How had his plans gone awry? It was time for plan B. The Wolf absolutely refused to allow the entire operation to unravel due to one inept underling. Nor would he easily give up control of the savage beast that lay untamed within his own spirit.

Commander Wilson must be the one at fault. The scientist continued to refuse all requests that he go willingly to the Middle East and continue with his research. The man should've understood it would be just a simple matter of allowing a different nation to foot his bills.

The commander had turned down offers that would've made him wildly wealthy. And he had successfully blocked all attempts at mind control, too.

Damn geniuses. His daughter had also found a way to block her thoughts from the Snake's control.

The Wolf poured himself a snifter of brandy and soothed his fragile temper with a sniff and then a swirl of the expensive amber-colored liquid.

At times he wished modern weapons could be used to force the Skinwalkers' will. But though the Brotherhood could use guns against the evil, the ancient text had been clear that the Skinwalkers' use of such things would cancel out all their gains.

But nothing should be allowed to alter the lifestyle he now led. He'd spent the first forty years of his life as a common man. But never again.

The brandy's rare flavor tasted more like the metallic promise of gold coins as it slithered down his throat. Now that he'd held a few of the ancient parchments in his hands, and knew the formula for gaining all power and wealth, nothing would ever turn him from the dark path.

This operation had taken too much effort, getting the Middle Easterners past the Immigration and Naturalization Service and hiding them from federal agents. He would give the Snake twelve hours to capture the daughter and get rid of the half-breed FBI agent.

At the thought of the half-breed, old blurred memories niggled into the Wolf's conscious mind. But he refused to allow them to intrude on his current thoughts. The Wolf would not tolerate sentiment of any kind. It had the potential for making him too human.

Not now. Not when he was so close to finalizing this deal for two-hundred-million dollars. The money would bring with it greater power and better chances for further gain.

Calming down, the Wolf decided to go back to the dinner table. One way or another, by lunch tomorrow the sheik would be wiring the money to the Skinwalkers' offshore accounts. If need be, he now knew Sheik Bashshar's mind would be easy enough to control. And there would be no further reason to deal with Commander Wilson or his daughter.

By any accounting, the money already belonged to the Skinwalkers. At the end of the day tomorrow the deal would be done. And so would the reasons to keep Commander Wilson alive.

Kody poked his head into the hospital room as he repeated sacred, healing chants in his mind. It was all he could do to put one foot in front of the other and come face-to-face with his mother as she lay in her hospital bed.

Audrey Long had never been physically sick a day in her life. And despite her depressed state since his father's death, Kody had just assumed his mother would be the steady rock of the family forever.

Suddenly, forever seemed like a lot less time than it had yesterday.

When he rounded the heavy door and quit counting the tiles on the floor long enough to lift his head, he stopped dead. He had asked Reagan to stay behind in the waiting room until he went to check on his mother.

But when he looked up, he was shocked to see that his mother already had a visitor. A man with a graying-blond mustache stood by her bedside. And he was holding her hand.

He was a tall white man who most certainly could not belong to the Big Medicine Clan, nor to any of their related clans. And he was a total stranger to Kody.

Something caught the stranger's attention. He looked over, and his green eyes took in Kody, who was standing at the threshold with his mouth hanging open in complete surprise.

"Ah," the stranger said softly. "The eldest son. Come closer, Agent Long. Your mother has been waiting to see you."

A hitch of irritation ran up Kody's back. Just who was this guy that he could be so familiar and order complete strangers around?

"My son?" His mother's weak voice made Kody snap to attention. He rushed to her bedside.

"I'll go grab something to eat," the stranger whispered to his mother in a gentle tone that grated on Kody. "But I won't be far. Have the nurses call me if you need anything while I'm gone."

Kody scowled at the man's back as he watched him leave. Then he returned his full attention to his mother, who was lying propped up in bed.

"What happened?" he growled. "And just who the hell was that guy, anyway?"

His mother's slight smile turned into a frown. "Have

you come to pay respects like my good son, or have you come to demand answers like a pushy lawman?"

"My mother…" he said with sigh of frustration. "I apologize for my rudeness. How is your health? Have the doctors told you the extent of your injuries?"

Her facial expression relaxed. "The worst of my injuries is a broken wrist," she said as she lifted her left arm so he could see the cast that went from knuckles to elbow. "But I have many bumps and bruises to try my patience."

"Mother," he said with another sigh. But this time the sigh came not from frustration but from the anguish of seeing her in pain. The hurt that erupted in his heart was surprisingly deep, and he could do nothing to ease it.

She motioned for him to come sit at the edge of her bed. He was hesitant, worrying that he might cause her further pain. But her smile widened and she nodded to indicate that it would be all right.

Kody sat and took her good hand in his own. "I'm so sorry. The rollover may have been all my fault."

"No. Not your fault. This was Skinwalker mischief."

"That's what I mean. I should've warned you to be more careful, or I should've been protecting you. At the very least, I should've stopped pushing to find Reagan's father."

"Ah. So you believe the Skinwalkers deliberately attacked me as a warning to you?"

He hadn't thought about it exactly like that. But now that she mentioned it, perhaps such an idea would be a logical conclusion. He gritted his teeth so the curse on the tip of his tongue would not offend his mother again.

But her smile grew weary. "Yes, I see that you do believe my injuries have something to do with the young woman and her father.

"My son, you must not stop your investigation in order to protect me. If you have the opportunity to halt the Skin-walkers' advancement, you must try. Their dark plague spreads daily."

"I can't compromise your safety."

"I will go to stay with my older sister near Farmington. If you discover that I must actually leave the land between the sacred four mountains to be safe, then our brother in Albuquerque will be happy to have his reservation relatives come for a visit."

"I'll take you to Farmington as soon as you are well enough to travel. Hopefully, you won't have to go too far from Dinetah."

His mother shook her head. "One of my nephews will take me to my sister's. Or perhaps our neighbor will agree to that favor. You and your brother are needed here."

"Has Hunter been to see you?" Kody was glad to think that someone from the Brotherhood would be taking his mother to her sister's. But he was rather surprised to hear that his own brother might've beat him to the hospital.

"My youngest son cannot bear to confront his mother's mortality. He still has much anger in his heart over his father's death. He will not come to me.

"But I know who my children are," she continued. "It does not matter that they cannot show it."

Kody closed his eyes and swiped a hand across his jaw. "I...I..." He couldn't get the words out.

Audrey Long reached up with her good hand and cupped his cheek. "Yes, my son. I know what you keep locked in your heart."

She put her hand on his shoulder and urged him to lean closer. Closer to her own heart.

"You must know how much you are loved by this old

woman," she whispered in his ear. "Your spirit has been in balance with my spirit from your first breath. That has not, and will not, ever change. Our spirits are intertwined forever."

She collapsed back against the pillows. "Please send in the young woman who has touched your heart. I wish to speak to her, and I grow tired."

Kody stood up and shook his head. "Reagan? But she hasn't touched—"

This time, his mother's smile was wry as she interrupted. "I'll tell you about the man you saw at my bedside. He is the doctor from Farmington who plans to perform surgery on my eyes when the time is right."

She patted the back of Kody's hand. "Your cousin, the crystal gazer, suggested a consultation nearly a year ago for my growing cataracts.

"The eye surgeon has touched your mother's spirit," she added. "There is no shame in acknowledging someone whose beauty sits in harmony with your own. It is the Navajo Way."

Kody was shocked. "You mean the two of you are…" He drew a breath and straightened his shoulders. "When my father died, you said you would never take another husband. Even though Dine tradition teaches that a spouse is to be taken in by the clan of the one who died."

"I said such a thing, yes. But following tradition was not possible. The one who died was Anglo and had no clan."

"So any single *bilagáana* man can take his place?"

"Your rudeness comes from surprise. And I have grown too tired to parry words with you." She patted his hand again and shook her head. "We will talk about this when I return. Now…please, send in your young woman."

Damn. Kody knew his words had been rude again. But hell. He'd just found out that his widowed mother had a boyfriend. How was he supposed to take such news?

Clamping down on his irritation, he gently touched his mother's cheek and then strode out of her room. Scowling and grumbling, Kody made his way down the hallway to seek out Reagan.

But she was definitely not *his* young woman. In fact, she was so far from being his that she might as well be the farthest star in the galaxy.

The image brought a grudging smile to his lips. Yes, Reagan was like a star, shining overhead and twinkling at all who really knew her.

There would be no chance to wish for her, however. No time nor future for wishes to be granted.

Reagan dragged a chair to Audrey Long's beside and waited for her to open her eyes. She had no idea what the older woman wanted to talk about. But Audrey had been so kind that Reagan would try her best to grant her anything.

"You love my son," Audrey said without opening her eyes to see who was really sitting beside her.

"What?" Reagan stared until the woman's eyes opened. "I…I…"

Audrey smiled. "You love my son." It was not a question; Kody's mother knew what she was talking about.

"Oh, well. I guess I do. But…"

"Yes, I understand," she said gently. "The situation is difficult. Most young lovers have hurdles to climb. It is the way of commitment and joining spirits."

Reagan figured she would be willing to climb just about anything to get Kody's love. But it was hopeless.

"My oldest son does not believe he is a person worthy

of love," Audrey said, as if reading her mind. "And he distrusts anyone who tries to break through the hard shell of his self-disgust."

She closed her eyes again but continued to talk. "After his father's death, he let anger and hatred push him to a dark place, and because of that he made many mistakes.

"But unlike my youngest son, Kody's anger has leeched out of his spirit after all these years. When the pain was fresh, Kody allowed it to fuel his determination to become a federal agent. One who could exact justice for his father's killers. He is a man who prefers action to prudence."

"Kody does seem to jump into things before he thinks them all the way through." Reagan's heart imagined that trait made him macho and exciting, though her mind knew how dangerous it could be.

Audrey moved her good arm out from under the covers and took Reagan's hand in hers. She looked up from under droopy eyelids.

"I keep your spirit in my heart, daughter. I believe you and my son shine under the same star. You also have grown to believe you are not worthy of being loved, as he has. But the strength you crave lives in your spirit and in your mind, not in the view of others.

"My son looks at you with love and balance," Audrey added. "Do not turn away because of the difficulties of circumstance or prejudice. I never regretted my mixed marriage."

Reagan shook her head in denial, but noticed that Kody's mother had already dropped off to sleep. The nurses had probably given her a sleeping pill earlier.

Easing her hand away from the older woman's, Reagan bit back selfish tears. She would gladly give up anything and face any prejudice if Kody loved her.

But his mother was seeing something in her son that was just not there. His feelings for Reagan probably ran not to love, but more toward friendship, duty or perhaps just lust.

Quietly standing and walking back to meet him, she wondered how she would ever be strong enough when the time came to leave the man who had stolen her heart.

Everyone kept saying she had a forceful, brilliant mind. But she wished to hurry up and find the courage that went along with it.

Chapter 16

*D*esperation.

Panicked, the Snake was so afraid of the consequences he would face from the Navajo Wolf if his efforts failed that he began to lose all control. The *bilagáana* daughter was too strong and courageous for him to overpower her mind.

There didn't seem to be any way of accomplishing the mission he had been assigned. And that would mean the end of his existence.

One last try. Once more, the Snake decided to directly attack the FBI agent. It had almost worked the last time. The foolish half-breed had turned his back and ended up swinging from a rope off the side of the cliff.

In his earliest childhood human persona, long before he turned Skinwalker, the Snake had known the half-breed. He remembered the young FBI agent as rash, at times even foolish, when it came to his own life.

If the Snake could manage to kill Kody Long, despite the Brotherhood's protection, then maybe the horror of witnessing his death would weaken the white woman enough to allow the Snake to capture her mind. Then both missions would be completed.

Yes, that seemed like his only hope.

It called for a surprise attack with no vibrations that would warn the Brotherhood. Such a thing was possible, but most difficult. It might drain all his power.

But as desperate as he was, that was a minor consideration. If the Snake was doomed to face death, then so was the half-breed lawman.

"That's it! I knew it."

"That's what?" For the last hour Kody had been driving them back toward his hogan in the pitch-black, moonless night. Clouds covered every source of light along the lonely highway. The dark was fathomless, like an empty crypt.

The naked eye could only take in a few short feet in front of their headlight beams. Yet Kody felt compelled to speed on through the night.

His worry over Reagan had been growing since they'd left the hospital. But he couldn't put his finger on the cause. Would the Skinwalkers try another attack while she rode in the truck and used her cell phone for text messaging? Her focus had been so concentrated on her call, he wondered if that made her an easier target.

But as he'd heard no telltale vibrations, Kody believed they were probably going to be okay. He kept a careful watch on the road and tried to disregard what his gut instincts were telling him.

"Well," Reagan began in answer to his earlier question.

"A friend of mine just found out what kind of project my father had been working on before he disappeared."

"Found out? Isn't that classified information?"

"Maybe."

He threw her a quick look that clearly told her not to try any bull.

"Okay. Yes, of course it's classified. But my friend can access any kind of info—online."

"A hacker? Into Navy Intelligence sites? Are you insane?" Kody knew he'd wiped the smile off her face by reminding her of the reality of the situation. But hell. Navy Intel?

"Just listen to what I found out," she said with clear irritation in her voice. "My father has developed something elegant and completely brand-new. A stealth helicopter. Isn't that wonderful? A discovery like that is a complete marvel of physics and engineering.

"And," she added, obviously thrilled at the idea, "it'll carry sixty field-equipped troops while flying fully loaded at thirty thousand feet, and can still easily avoid appearing on anyone's radar."

"Sweet," he said with a nod. "But that's the kind of project most evildoers, and many aggressive nations, would pay big bucks to get their hands on."

She turned her head with a quick grin. "Yeah, it is. In fact, the Pentagon is convinced my dad has taken his plans to Russia or China.

"Apparently, blog rumors have been flying, hinting that maybe India or Pakistan have already made offers. I guess the POB aren't even looking for him in the U.S."

"POB. Powers that be. Hmm. Your online friend has access to privileged Pentagon memos, too?"

Reagan hesitated a second before answering. "As long

as the memos were sent or stored on a computer that has Internet capabilities, yes he does."

Kody let a long, low whistle say what he thought of that kind of criminal behavior. But Reagan's hands were waving dismissively.

"No one will ever know who or why. Don't worry. But I'm wondering if we shouldn't notify the FBI or maybe the CIA of our suspicions about the Skinwalkers kidnapping my father. Or should we go directly to Homeland Security?"

"Absolutely not." Kody almost shouted the words. "I don't know how the evil ones fit into the picture, exactly, but they're smack in the middle of it for sure.

"It hasn't been very long since you refused to believe in the concept of Skinwalkers," Kody added with a raised eyebrow he knew she probably didn't see in the dark. "What would the unimaginative bureaucrats at 'Home' think if you tried explaining it to them?"

Reagan was lost in thought for a few seconds. "Okay, I can accept that. We'll leave it to your Brotherhood.

"I know the coordinates now," she added. "I just need another minute or two on the computer to plug them into the formula, and we should have a ninety-five percent probability on the point of origin. This is such a beautiful equation."

The equation wasn't nearly as beautiful as its creator. Kody pushed his foot down harder on the gas pedal. They needed to find a safe place for her to access a computer.

A thunder roll drummed across the midnight sky. Just as it had the night the two of them had spent in the ancient ruin, a storm was coming in over the Lukachukais.

Kody reached for his cell phone and punched up his brother's number on speed dial. But before the connection could be made, something altered the atmosphere, both inside and outside of the truck's cab. It seemed as if they had entered a different world, an electrified one where time crawled to a stop and reality went berserk.

There had been no warning vibration, but on pure instinct, Kody slammed on the brakes and dropped his cell phone on the floor without disconnecting the call in order to keep both hands firmly on the wheel.

As the pickup swerved and slowed, the right shoulder of the road suddenly seemed to drop off into a black abyss—or maybe it was just a deep, dark ditch. Either way, he didn't want the truck to end up there.

Something leaped out of the ditch at them, and Kody's heart stopped. It was black and slimy and big. Big enough to be at eye level with the cab window.

The monstrous creature hovered there a moment, glaring at them. Its yellow eyes glowed and grew darker, blackened by evil. Then its silver tongue whipped out and grabbed on to the roof with one loud hiss and little effort. Kody could feel the truck tipping on its side and skidding toward the ditch.

"Kody!" Reagan yelled.

His panic for her safety turned to frozen horror as he realized he had let her down. They'd been ambushed, and there was no way he could save her now.

"Kody," she repeated, grabbing his arm. "Remember the chants. Say them."

"Huh?"

"Say the chants," she insisted. "Now."

Reagan saw her words finally registering across Kody's features. For some unaccountable reason, the evil presence had not terrified her one bit. She wasn't sure how she knew it, but no matter how horrific the Skinwalker snake seemed at this moment, it could be beaten.

If Kody could manage to hold it off with the Brotherhood's sacred chants for a few minutes, long enough for her to focus, she might be able to make use of the mind connection the snake had opened between them days ago. She had visions of making the creature retreat by using concentration and control.

Kody began reciting the singsong Navajo words, slowly and quietly at first. Then, when terror's icy fingers finally loosened the hold they'd apparently had on his mind, his chanting became louder and much stronger.

Since the day they'd met, Reagan had known her love was the most courageous man in the world. Now she had proof.

The black evil hissed again, and the sound rushed through her. But she would not allow it to break her concentration. This damn entity was not nearly intelligent enough to stop her now.

A few chanted words and the truck was freed. The old pickup settled back solidly on all four wheels.

She pushed open the passenger door as fast as she could and slid down to stand on the dirt shoulder. Facing an eight-foot-long snake that was coiling and getting ready to strike, she was madder than hell.

How dare this *thing* try to hurt Kody!

The serpent glared at her in the wavering illumination of the headlights. She should've been afraid. But she could hear its panicked thoughts in her mind exactly as though it was speaking aloud.

Desperation. I must win. Kill. It is the half-breed's life or mine.

In her own more steady thoughts, Reagan made it clear to the formidable reptile that she had no intention of losing a battle of wills. "You won't kill. Back off."

Cannot. A strangled gargle came from its midsection.

The snake slithered a few feet away, then stopped and quickly recoiled, giving every appearance of readying itself for another attack.

Behind her, she heard Kody opening the driver's side door and calling her name. "Reagan, move away."

He'd stopped saying the chants aloud. But he couldn't stop yet! She closed her eyes and concentrated all her efforts on making the snake go away, though her growing fear for Kody's life refused to be denied. The terrifying image of his death was ruining her focus.

The snake hissed again and she felt the lick of its tongue at her legs. With a slash, it tore through her jeans and stung her flesh. She dropped to her knees.

"Dammit!" Kody's strangled voice behind her caused a sharp pain in her gut. She had failed him.

Another loud cracking noise assailed her ears. Please no! Not Kody!

Her eyes popped open just in time to see the snake exploding into a thousand pieces of inky confetti. The acrid smell of sulfur was strong.

But as she turned to find Kody, she realized it wasn't sulfur she was smelling, but gunpowder. With his weapon drawn, Special Agent Long moved around the front of the truck to fire yet another bullet directly into the snake's limp form.

After a second's inspection of what had been the serpent, Kody dropped the gun back into his shoulder holster and ran toward her. He knelt and gathered her in his arms.

"Where are you hurt, Red? Are you bleeding?"

She sat back on the pavement, stretched out her legs and rolled up her jeans. Angry welts marked where the creature's tongue had whipped her shins, but there didn't seem to be any blood.

"I don't think so. Are *you* all right?"

Kody's shoulders relaxed and he took a breath. "I'm just terrific, thanks. What the hell were you thinking? You could've been killed."

"Good question, bro." The sound of Hunter's voice came out of the mist. "What were you two doing out here at this hour without the Brotherhood to watch your backs?"

The man she loved didn't turn around to answer his brother. Hunter shrugged and walked over to check the inert figure on the ground, while Kody lifted Reagan in his arms and carried her toward the pickup.

"We did okay." He finally answered Hunter's question in a roundabout manner.

"Doesn't seem that way to me," Hunter said with a sly grin. "But I suppose it *is* the evil one who lies dead in the dirt and not my older brother. So…"

"Is there a body?" Reagan asked over Kody's shoulder as she nestled in his arms. "I thought I saw the snake explode."

"The human form of the Skinwalker is intact and familiar to the Brotherhood." Hunter nodded to her in a subtle Navajo-style move. "Bahe Douglas leaves no immediate family, but his clan will need many healing ceremonies to cleanse his spirit from their destinies."

"Douglas? The trading post owner was a Skinwalker?"

"Seems so."

Reagan wasn't interested in how they'd missed guessing who had been the Skinwalker. She was much more curious about how it had died, and in the unique transformation of the dead snake back into human form—all the scientific, geeky stuff she loved.

"I didn't know these Skinwalkers could be killed with a gun," she said to Kody. "I mean, I imagined it would take something special. Like a…like a…"

"Like a stake through the heart, Red?" Kody was smiling as he slid her into the pickup's passenger seat. "Or maybe with garlic? Sorry. We don't have any vampires in Navajoland. At least not to my knowledge.

"Skinwalkers are bad enough," he added. "And right now, all I care about is getting you safely home. So how about buckling up and leaving Hunter to deal with this particular Skinwalker's last journey?"

"Fine. I'm sorry I saved your life. Is that what you wanted to hear?" Several hours had passed and Kody was frantically searching for just the right thing to say to let Reagan know how afraid he'd been for her—without *saying* it in so many words.

They were safe and sound again in his hogan. She sat at his computer, studiously plugging GPS coordinates into her program, while he fumbled in the kitchen, warming up some of his mother's packaged food.

Reagan had wanted to know why he'd been so quick to pull the trigger on the snake, when neither of them had seemed to be in imminent danger. It wouldn't be terribly smart to open himself up to potential pain. Just the thought of telling her how desperate he'd been to keep her safe— or of how paralyzed with fear he'd been when he was sure there was nothing he could possibly do to help her—made his throat contract.

Hell, no. Saying any of that didn't seem like a good idea at all.

The beautiful woman with a genius mind who was now sitting at his computer had actually stood between him and the Skinwalker—without giving a single thought to her own safety.

But her safety was all he had been able to think of at the time.

She was much more courageous than he was, and would never understand if he tried to tell her about his darkest hours spent cowering in indecision. Worse yet, when her father was finally located, she would be leaving Dinetah for good. Better that she leave a little aggravated at him than be tempted to look back.

But when he glanced over, she was staring up at him with huge luminous eyes full of tears. Had the words he'd thrown at her without thinking put that devastated expression across those fascinating features?

He walked to her side, feeling like a first-class bastard. "Reagan? You know I didn't mean what I said the way it came out. Right?"

She shook her head but didn't reply.

Crouching down beside her, Kody searched for a way to make her understand. "I realize, admittedly a little late, that you wanted to try putting ideas into the snake's brain. But as brave as you were, I couldn't let—"

"Me? Brave?" She interrupted him with a self-depreciating laugh. "No way. I was scared to death. But I truly believe if you'd kept saying the chants for a few more moments, I would've found out what the Skinwalkers have done with my father."

Yeah. It wasn't the first time he'd screwed up because he'd been too focused on himself and his own concerns. But he had to hope that this time it wouldn't cost Reagan her father's life.

"Listen to me, Red. I—"

She shook her head. "I can't listen."

"Why not?"

"Because I love you and that makes me lose control," she rasped. "When you talk, I can't think straight. That snake wanted *you,* not me, and I couldn't let anything—"

"Hold it. Back up a second. You love me?"

She turned her face away and dropped her chin. For a second he wasn't sure he'd heard her right. But then she sighed heavily and nodded.

His chest tightened and breathing became difficult. Somewhere deep in his soul, he'd wanted her to care—to give a damn about a half-breed with lots of family and not a single soul who thought he really mattered.

His mother had certainly mouthed the right words at the hospital, but she couldn't have meant what she'd said. Not after some of the things he'd done.

And as for Reagan loving him... It was all wrong. They would never be able to work out their problems.

"You can't," he finally spat. "Don't love me. I'm not worthy of being loved...by anyone. Once, long ago, I faced a test that might've made me a man worth a few tears and promises, but I failed. And because of my failure, my father is gone for good."

"Your father? But I thought..."

"Yeah. He died eleven years ago. Back then, he hadn't told the family, but he was being stalked by an old adversary. He didn't realize the guy had found him on the rez. The tribal police received a tip and they tried to contact him, but he was out in the field.

"Those were the days before cell phone reception was decent in Dinetah, so they gave me the message. But I couldn't be bothered to cancel my activities long enough to go search out my father. By the time my basketball pickup game was over, Dad had already disappeared.

"They found him in his burned out car a week later at the bottom of a four-hundred-foot ravine. His body was incinerated beyond recognition, but they found a bullet lodged in what remained of his skull. It had been no accident."

"But that couldn't have been your fault," Reagan said. "You didn't know, and your father was a lawman. He should've been able to protect himself. Or the tribal police should've sent someone else out to warn him. You were only a kid. There was no way you could've been expected to—"

He waved aside her objections. "In my head I know the truth, but in my heart I'm still at fault. I joined the Brotherhood when I discovered they were at war against the Skinwalkers. I'd hoped it might bring me back into harmony and help erase the worst of my past.

"I vowed at the beginning that I would not take another wife. It was a sensible promise. A man becomes too vulnerable when he cares about…"

Oh hell. Of course. With a sudden blinding insight, Kody realized he already cared too much about Reagan. When it had been her life at stake, he was the one who'd dropped his guard and became vulnerable to attack…just as he had been warned he would if he let himself become involved.

But he wanted Reagan to know there was more than one reason there couldn't be a future for the half-breed and the genius. "Believe me, even if I was free, people would be quick to tell you you're crazy to love a half-breed. There are those on both sides who can be cruel. Ask my ex-wife."

Reagan jerked her head around and narrowed her eyes at him. "Stop that. Do you think I care about what other people say? If I did, I'd spend my whole life in tears over being called a geeky nerd—both to my face and behind my back.

"I've just been fooling myself, wanting to believe I might've been worthy of being loved," she whispered. "Of having someone like you care about me."

Kody didn't fully listen to every word she said because he got lost when he heard her tear herself down. She was so gorgeous and so smart—and so sexy. He took her by the shoulders and pressed his mouth hard against the silky texture of her lips to quiet her.

He quieted her all right. But he also managed to make himself nuts with desire.

He touched her lips with his tongue and she opened for him. Ah. The flavors of her were as he remembered…and yet so much more.

She tasted of coffee and honey, and something so vivid and spicy that he became instantly addicted and aroused.

The kiss went on and on. Kody figured he could stay right here with her, kissing her, for eternity maybe.

But as the heat between them exploded in his gut, fiery passion clouded his mind. Operating on instinct and pure lust, he only recognized the desperation. Practical matters had all disappeared.

He was driven to feel the texture of her skin beneath his fingers. Needed to slide back into her tight, slick warmth and bury all his insecurities until they disappeared from his mind in a savage fury of red desire.

His lust took charge of the situation and tipped the scales out of balance. He'd gone beyond all Navajo subtlety, slipping his hands beneath the edge of her shirt.

Gliding up the fine, satin skin of her rib cage and taking pleasure in the feel of her body, he came in contact with the underside of her breasts. His fingers hesitated as he

touched material every bit as soft as her skin. In his cliff
dream, he'd expected sensible cotton from his sensational
genius lover....

Sudden images from that first night with the bees
sneaked up on him. Back then, he'd stripped her and discovered she'd worn a lacy black bra and panties. Those
pictures in his head snapped the last thread of civilized
behavior remaining from all his Navajo training.

The beast that lurked within every man took over.

Chapter 17

When Kody's fingers came in contact with her bra, Reagan felt his hesitation. She stifled a groan and nipped at his bottom lip, urging him on.

He couldn't stop now. Not when the heat from his touch was skittering down her chest and landing at her core.

And not when this might be her last opportunity to experience the kind of explosion that only he could ignite. Tonight should probably be the end. Once she found her father, there would be no reason to spend many more hours with Kody. So her frantic desire needed to be soothed with one final goodbye.

Encouraging him to lift her T-shirt, she arched her back and moaned. She craved one last chance to memorize the way he smelled. The way he made those hungry little sounds when she squirmed against his mouth. And the way he stared at her body as if she was some kind of goddess instead of a plain woman with loads of faults.

He tenderly messaged her breasts through the silk of her bra, while she worried that maybe they should stop before things went too far. Another taste of happiness and she might never recover. How could she walk away now that she knew the yin and yang of how he could be?

Perhaps when the end came, he would try to make it easier on himself by turning his back on her. Fully expecting her to be smart enough to keep her chin high and start walking.

Could he be so selfish? Or would that really be kind?

The conflicts were making her crazy.

As he rolled a nipple between his thumb and forefinger, she relished the sensation, while her gut was busy trying to convince her mind that she would have to be the strong one of the two in the end. He had made a vow, and she couldn't let him go back on that even if he wanted to.

Only just now, after eleven years, was he beginning to forgive himself for his father's death. Kody hadn't told her that in so many words, but she knew it as surely as she knew the warm brown color of his eyes.

She could never live with herself if he turned away from his family, his heritage and his vows in order to be with her. Was she crazy to even want such a thing?

Reagan pushed away from him, wiggled her T-shirt back into place and crossed her arms over her breasts. "I'm really close to finding the right coordinates for the Skinwalker point of origin. Can I take a rain check with you until after we locate my father?"

Man. That might've been the hardest thing she had ever forced herself to do or say. Especially now that Kody's sensual expression was being replaced by a cold dark glare.

He swiped the back of a hand across his mouth and stood up, towering over her. "Sure. No problem. Finish your work." Turning, he started back toward the tiny kitchen.

But halfway there he turned around and came back to stand beside her again. "We'll find your father, Reagan. And with your coordinates to guide us, I'm sure we'll make it before they can move him off Navajoland. They need him alive and well. He's still okay."

Cupping her cheek, he gazed down at her with an expression that was hard to define. No one had ever looked at her that way. Kody seemed to be seeing her as if she were some kind of priceless jewel, instead of a heartless bitch who'd turned him away.

But she was feeling pretty worthless at the moment. Making him stop what they were doing a minute ago had ended up being the biggest lie she had ever told.

And she wanted to take it all back. Too late.

It had been an hour since Reagan had pinpointed a five-mile radius around the trading post, and they were now on their way there. But Kody was having trouble keeping his mind on driving.

Harmony and balance be damned. His Anglo side was overpowering his Navajo conditioning.

Revenge and anger were not part of the typical Navajo's training. Any man who had done wrong, even a criminal who had injured you, was not someone to hate. Rather, such a man was simply out of control. A person to be pitied and corrected, brought back into balance, not punished.

Well, sorry. Kody was just plain furious that some Skin-walker or some terrorist somewhere was holding Reagan's father's future in his hands.

It would destroy her if they didn't reach him in time to save his life. She had everything, all her dreams for a family, riding on a man she barely knew. He had been hovering in her life, but had never really been there for her.

In her mind and her dreams, she had made the commander out to be the cure for all her loneliness.

And Kody knew he would spend the rest of eternity in hell, wishing he had done things differently, if he failed to save that dream for her.

Gripping the steering wheel in white-knuckled fists, he kept most of his attention on the rutted, mud-slick road that he'd used as a shortcut. But he managed to glance toward Reagan in the passenger seat.

With her handheld wireless turned to GPS positioning and her maps in her lap, she was focused on the task—even as the truck lurched and jostled across potholes, throwing her forward against the seat belt. He knew he needed to maintain some of that same focus.

Stop daydreaming about a future that will not be, and keep your mind on the job. But he couldn't help thinking of what a life with Reagan would've been like. How full of color and passion she was. How she'd turned out to be everything he hadn't even known he'd wanted.

His cell phone came to life on the dashboard and he answered the call with a jerk of his hand.

"The Bird People have joined the hunt, brother," Hunter blurted out, without bothering to announce himself. "They have your pickup in sight."

"Ask them to help search the area surrounding Three

Eagles Trading Post. But don't let anyone else spot you. We'll meet you there in ten minutes."

"Anyone who?" Hunter asked. "Except for Commander Wilson, who and what are we looking for?"

"I'm not sure. Look for a place near the trading post where they could've hidden the commander in plain sight." Kody chided himself for not having thought of the place as soon as the snake had turned out to be Bahe Douglas. Why had it taken Reagan to locate the spot?

Another sharp look at her and Kody had his answer. Keeping her safe—or safely in his arms—had been his entire focus.

Kody swallowed back the fear that they might not get there in time. He considered calling in the FBI, but decided to hold off until he knew more about the situation they would find.

It seemed he'd actually learned a little something from Reagan last night. Gaining patience was a good thing.

Absently, he wondered how he'd missed that lesson from his Navajo conditioning. Waiting for the right information was smart. But the dread of losing this particular battle had already sneaked up, and stood poised to throw him into a panic.

"He's going to be okay." The sound of Reagan's voice broke into his thoughts.

"Huh?"

"I know you were right and he'll still be there." She laid a hand over her heart. "I feel it in here."

It was good that she felt optimistic, wasn't it? Or would it be better if she was prepared for the worst? Kody's twin cultures were split on which way was best.

So he kept his mouth shut and kept driving.

The cell phone jangled to life again.

"The Bird People say the only possibility in that area is a double-wide trailer about two hundred yards behind the trading post." This time it was Lucas Tso on the phone. His voice, too, was easy to recognize.

"It's hidden in a cedar grove about a half mile north from your position," Lucas continued. "According to the birds, you picked the right road, cousin. It'll take you within walking distance as soon as you top the next hill. But there's no movement near the trailer. You sure this is the place to look for the missing Anglo?"

Kody turned the question over to Reagan, who nodded. "No question about it. Unless they've already taken him out of the country, the numbers don't lie."

Kody responded to Lucas and clicked off the phone, then put his foot on the brake. He didn't want the noise of the pickup to alert whoever was inside the trailer. It would be better if he parked and walked over the hill.

Pulling off the gravel road near a culvert, Kody shut down the ignition and reached for his weapons. He checked and holstered the Glock and then opened the door so he could pull the shotgun from its spot behind the seat.

Reagan opened her door, too.

"Hold it, Red. You stay with the truck."

She shook her head and he almost got lost again in the rusty-colored flash of curls swirling like a halo around her head. "Don't go alone. You might need my help." She hesitated and looked stricken by what she'd said. "I mean, that's my father in there. I should go along so he won't be afraid. I could help…."

Kody waited patiently until she wound down, but he was secretly thrilled that she didn't want him to go into danger without her. "You can't help, Red. That is, unless you're an expert marksman and haven't told me about it yet."

Scowling, she stuck out her bottom lip. "No. No gun training. But I'm a fast learner."

"Right." The bark of laughter left his mouth before he could hold it back. "I'll be a lot safer if I'm not worrying about you. Plus, you're going to be needed here anyway. Stay and man the phone. While I do recon, you and I can text message each other. I'll let you know what to tell the Brotherhood."

"Oh. Well, okay. I guess I can do that," she reluctantly agreed.

He realized she wasn't happy to stay behind, but damn, she was spectacular. He dipped his chin at her and winked. And she blushed. The sight of that rosy flush spreading across places he would love to revisit almost stopped the entire rescue operation.

"Kody…"

"Yeah, Red. I know. I'll be careful." He backed away from the truck and eased the door closed.

There was more he would've said, but it would have to wait until he brought her father back to safety. And by then, it would probably be too late.

Kody moved silently up a barren, rocky hill, trying to scout out a good vantage point. The gray cast of dawn was slowly giving way to the violets and magentas of daybreak. But he didn't have time to stop and admire the spectacular sunrise.

When he hit the crest of the hill, he found a boulder the size of Arizona to hide behind as he scanned the terrain.

Directly below him, a few aspens and a cluster of stunted ponderosa pines partially obscured his view. Right past them was a small grove of salt cedars that must be sheltering the trailer.

Moving fast to beat the dawn, Kody crossed the open space between the aspens and pines to a spot just inside the cedar grove, where he had direct access to the trailer. From his place, only fifty feet behind the half-hidden double-wide, he had a good view of two sides of it.

He leaned the shotgun against a tree and pulled out both his cell phone and foldaway binoculars. Just then, a light switched on inside the trailer, and the nearby sound of swishing wings reminded him that he was not alone.

A quick glance upward told him that several raptors were circling above his head. The red-shouldered and zone-tailed hawks seemed to be waiting for instructions.

Several seconds later, he had the binoculars strapped around his neck, and the cell phone open and set for text messaging. He hit Reagan's speed dial number and asked her to relay to the Bird People a request to keep watch on the sides of the trailer he couldn't see.

She answered in the affirmative and added, R U OK?

It made him smile. OK. U stay safe.

Her message came back. Bro ETA 5 mins tops. Wait.

Which sounded like good advice, except that right then a door opened onto a small deck and a man's head ducked out. His body shortly followed, but then he turned back and began dragging another man out of the trailer by the arm.

Kody focused his binoculars but it really wasn't necessary. The second man was obviously Reagan's father. His thinning wisps of auburn hair were a dead giveaway.

It was pretty easy to tell that Commander Wilson had

been drugged. His eyes were glazed and his head and shoulders slumped as he shuffled along.

The other man was far more interesting to Kody at the moment. He was short, wiry and dark skinned. And he had a .45 strapped to his waist that was big enough to blow the head off a grizzly.

But he was not a Navajo. Not a Skinwalker.

Maybe they would get lucky and find that the evil ones had left Commander Wilson in the custody of the Middle Eastern terrorist group. Terrorists would be easier to overpower. They couldn't change from human form. They couldn't fly away. And the FBI would gladly round them up.

Kody couldn't wait for the cavalry to save the day. The dark-skinned man forced Commander Wilson to sit down at an outdoor table. He said something that Kody couldn't hear, then reached over, clapped a set of handcuffs on Reagan's father and went back inside.

This might just be the best chance they had for a rescue. When else could they be sure of catching Commander Wilson alone? Kody didn't want to risk waiting for the Brotherhood or the FBI.

He clipped the cell phone back on his belt and eased his knife from its sheath as he crouched and ran for the nearest corner of the trailer. Gluing himself flat against the siding, he took inventory of his surroundings. There was only one window along this side, and a short set of stairs separated him from Reagan's father and the answer to her prayers.

Silently, stealthily, Kody inched along the wall toward the deck. Reaching the window, he ducked and crawled underneath. Another few feet and he could reach out and touch the commander.

Taking one more quiet step, he suddenly stopped

when he heard a noise behind him—the sound of a bullet being chambered.

He swung around, sent his knife flying toward its target and threw himself on the ground—just as the bullet whizzed over his head.

Reagan was hiding behind a cedar tree, text messaging with the Brotherhood, when she heard the sound of a gun exploding. Kody?

She didn't waste a second before calling the FBI. Good thing she'd stored their direct number in her Blackberry. Explaining that she was calling at Kody's request, she answered their questions quickly and accurately. Agent Long would've been proud.

During the whole conversation, Reagan kept moving through the trees toward the last place she'd spotted Kody. She'd followed him earlier because she'd been terrified for him.

Hesitating behind a tree at the edge of the grassy yard next to the trailer, Reagan hung up with the FBI and tried to catch her breath. Where was Kody? She couldn't see anything from this position.

Did she dare sneak any closer? Damn straight she would. Taking one small step into the open, Reagan was stunned when someone grabbed her by the arm and dragged her back to the sheltering shade of the tree trunk.

Ohmigod. One of the terrorists?

She spun around, ready to kick and scratch. But Hunter stood there, shushing her while at the same time working his own cell phone in silent text messaging.

Finally he stopped for a second. "There aren't enough of us to rush them. The Brotherhood has the place surrounded, but the bad guys have barricaded themselves inside. Not sure, but I think there's about six of them."

"The FBI is on the way," she whispered. "Where's Kody? Is he…?"

Hunter smiled and raised one eyebrow. "You called in the feds? How long ago?"

"A few minutes. Please. Is Kody all right?"

"Looked fit as ever to me. He almost managed to take out one of the terrorists. Winged the guy's shooting arm. But it was up to me to finish the job when that half-dead terrorist rose up a few minutes later and took a bead on my brother's back…using his left arm."

She gasped and tried to drag in air.

"Kody's headed back to the pickup with your father," Hunter hurriedly told her.

The distant sound of helicopters suddenly interrupted their quiet conversation. Hunter looked skyward, then flipped open his cell phone and sent a message.

In a minute he turned to her again. "You haven't left yet? The Bird People say there are enough FBI agents headed this way to take care of everything. I don't think you want to be here when they arrive.

"Wouldn't you rather check on your father?" he added.

Reagan gave a start, then smiled. "Is the Brotherhood waiting for the bad guys to be rounded up?"

"The Bird People have volunteered to remain and keep the terrorists contained until the feds take over," Hunter told her with a solemn nod. "There are many other places where the rest of us can be useful today."

That was all she needed to hear. She quickly started back through the trees toward Kody and her father.

The FBI would come and arrest the terrorists simply

because they were here illegally. And the feds would never even know about the Brotherhood's role in finding them. Or about one Navy commander who had been kidnapped during his vacation on the reservation.

Chapter 18

"Dad's fine this morning," Reagan told Kody two days later. "The drugs are almost out of his system."

"Sheik Bashshar's health seems better today, too," he replied. "But I understand *he's* roaring mad. Claims he lost several hundred million dollars to a weird guy who sometimes has fangs and pointed ears."

Kody couldn't stop the chuckle. "The story he's telling is so twisted, I don't think the Bureau will ever connect your father to any of it."

"What does the FBI have to say about his story?"

He raised his eyebrows. "They're nodding and taking notes, but they don't say much. In fact, my supervisor says the Washington big shots are racing through paperwork trying to get him and his buddies into a detention camp. Should be some interesting interrogations there."

Reagan looked so beautiful this morning with the

sunshine adding scarlet highlights to her hair. He wanted to hold her, to soothe her the way he had before. But he sensed she wouldn't be receptive to him. That harsh knowledge took a hammer to his balance.

"Dad called his C.O.," she said with a small shrug. "I'm going back to White Sands with him today so he can surrender. I'm not sure how much trouble he's in, because he has the plans back in his possession…all thanks to you."

"Getting the plans out of that trailer is all thanks to the Bird People. The FBI wasn't ready for the whole truth. They never even realized what happened."

Kody knew because he'd called in to his field office a few minutes ago. He'd planned to go back to work today himself. But all that could change, if…

"Do you want me to come with you, Red? I could act as a witness. Or I could—"

Reagan shook her head. "I don't think it's a good idea." She hesitated, refusing to look at him. "Listen, the Dine need you here. You've made vows to the Brotherhood."

She didn't want him with her? Kody felt a sharp pain in the vicinity of his heart. But he steeled himself to show nothing.

"Yeah," he managed to grunt past his closed throat. "So will you come back after you get your dad settled?"

This time she turned around and spoke over her shoulder. "No, that's not such a hot idea, either. An Anglo woman doesn't belong here. You said so yourself."

He took her shoulders and gently tugged her around until she was facing him. "I may have been wrong," he rasped. "My father was an Anglo married to one of the People and he fit in okay. Others do it, too."

She was slowly shaking her head now and the panic

built in his gut. "Reagan, come back to me. Don't walk away. We have something. I—I…"

"You can't break your vow," she said with a half sob. "If you did, I'm afraid you would grow to hate yourself…and you'd end up hating me, too."

He dropped his hands to his sides in defeat. Damned if she wasn't right—as usual.

But he couldn't possibly let her go without giving her a piece of his spirit. Something to remember on cold, cruel nights. He had dozens of images of her to hold on to through the passage of time, but she might not even remember him next week.

Hoping he could get the meaning across in a coherent enough manner, he decided that including a few vaguely remembered lines from an old Native American poem wouldn't hurt. Those words would say what he really felt so much better than he ever could.

"I will stay with my clan and be true to my heritage as I promised," Kody began, taking her hand. "But I want you to know that I'll always be with you, too. When you hear the rain falling on the ground, take a look around. I'll be there. I will be the wind in your hair, the sunshine on your face…the beating of your heart during a thunderstorm. That will be me."

Kody looked into her eyes and saw tears and realized he was causing her pain. He couldn't stand hurting her.

He dropped her hand and stepped back. "From now on, you will never be alone again. Someone will always be walking beside you, Red. Forever."

Then he turned and did the hardest thing he'd ever attempted. He walked away from the only person that could've saved him from a lifetime of loneliness.

* * *

"You have lost your harmony, brother." Hunter sat at the wide kitchen table at their cousin's hogan, shaking his head in that slight, almost imperceptible Navajo way.

"Is this meeting about me?" Kody demanded irritably.

Lucas Tso tilted his chin slightly in answer. "It has been a month since the computer woman left Dinetah. Since then you have developed a sickness of the heart. But what you have cannot be cured by any ancient medicine or chants."

Kody felt the fury building in his chest. Members of the Brotherhood were smart and he was loyal to them. But they had no right to tell him…

"Listen with your heart and not your head, cousin." Dr. Ben Wauneka spoke in low tones but with steely determination. "There are many ways for the evil ones to win without lifting a finger. We cannot stand silent and watch one of our own be felled without a shot."

Kody had great respect for his cousin Ben, but this was butting in where he had no business. "Look. I might be a little off balance, but I'll turn it around. It just takes time. You can't rush these things."

Dammit. He really hoped that what he'd just said was the truth. Losing Reagan was killing him. His life seemed like walking death without her.

"A warrior cannot ask for more time from an enemy," Michael Ayze interjected. "The greatest break for the evil ones is your loss of concentration and harmony. With you as a weak link, the Brotherhood will be lost."

"You want me to leave the Brotherhood?" Kody was astounded. Could they really be kicking him out?

Hunter smiled. "You are too good a warrior to lose, Bro. The Brotherhood needs more warriors, not less."

"More?"

"Sit down, cousin. We have a proposition to put to you," Ben said with an ironic smile. "The answer to your sickness lies with Reagan Wilson. That is clear to all. And we need you here, to fight the evil ones."

Kody sat down and rested his chin on his fist. "Yeah. But she's already rejected my—"

Hunter shook his head and interrupted. "Hear us out. We were impressed by her computer work and text messaging at Three Eagles. The Brotherhood needs to use modern methods. The Skinwalkers have proved that though they are using ancient powers, they are also using advanced technology to stay ahead of us."

"What are you saying?"

"We would like your woman to join our side in the war," Lucas said. "Her genius will make for a more even fight."

"What?" He was stunned. Would she? Could she?

"She thinks the People won't accept her, that you…" Lucas waved his hands. "The woman is too smart to believe in that. She spoke those words with no meaning in order to give you a way out. Ask again."

"I don't…I'm not sure she'll believe me. If you want her in the Brotherhood, couldn't one of you ask?"

Hunter smiled again. "You must ask her yourself. But, yes, we have also prepared the way."

"Huh?"

"Our birth mother and the one who gave birth to the Brotherhood are traveling to your woman now. They will prepare her for clan life. She will be expected to join the family."

"Mother and Shirley Nez? They left Dinetah?"

"Your woman has been staying in Albuquerque with her father. Our mother and Shirley will be meeting with her in their brother's hogan there. Don't worry. The elders will be safe with their clan, and they don't mind being *modern* for Reagan's sake."

"Oh." Now Kody was nearly speechless. But a tiny spurt of hope began to grow in his gut.

It might work. Maybe. Reagan was definitely the kind to feel a strong responsibility to do good work, and to be loyal to a cause. Wasn't she the one who had reminded him of his vows?

"How soon will you leave?" The question came from Michael Ayze, who had been sitting quietly in a shadowed corner.

"Leave?"

"Go now," Hunter demanded. "The sooner you have full concentration again, the sooner the Brotherhood will be back in harmony and ready to do battle."

Yes, Kody agreed silently as he stood and checked off the moves it would take to get himself and his vehicle ready to travel the three hundred miles to Albuquerque. Now was the best time to find out whether his life could be put back in balance. Or whether he was doomed to forever wander as only half a man.

Reagan quietly sipped her tea, hoping the two older women wouldn't see how badly her hands were shaking. They looked so solemn, almost scary. Why had they invited her to visit with them? Had she done something wrong? Broken some taboo?

For the last month, she had been checking regularly on Mrs. Long's health—first in the hospital and then by calling her after she had been released. Reagan knew the sweet woman was healing, almost miraculously. Her bruising was completely gone and she was down to a removable, temporary cast on the wrist.

Thinking of Kody's mother and how kind she was gave Reagan a warm feeling. Unfortunately, the feeling was followed by a hollow thump in her chest. It had been a long month of tears for Reagan, aching for the man she had left behind.

Many times she'd caught herself wishing that Mrs. Long was her own mother. How different her life would've been if only she'd had someone that kind and easy to talk to in her own family.

Family? Ha. That was a misnomer if there ever was one. Reagan had no real family. Just people who were related to her by genes and money.

Her dad had turned out to be a good person, of course. And had also turned out to be a lot like her. But maybe that was the problem. He was too much like her. A genius, surely. But scatterbrained and so focused on science and computers that he had very little real life. Reagan had finally figured out how he could've gone for all those years not knowing that his wife was taking drugs.

"How is your birth father, my daughter?" Mrs. Long asked, as if reading her mind.

"He's well, thank you. The Navy inquiry into his actions is finished. They've decided to have him quietly retire from the service.

"He'll be continuing with his work, however," Reagan added. "The country needs his ideas. But he'll be working as a government-contracted consultant. My guess is Navy security will plan to stick much closer to him in the future."

"Will that be troublesome for him?" Shirley asked.

"No. I doubt if he'll even notice the difference."

"And how is your work?" Mrs. Long asked. "Have you extended your leave of absence?"

Reagan shook her head slowly. This was the first time since she'd decided on her new future that she would be faced with explaining herself to someone else. Her life was so very different now than it had been before she'd come to the reservation looking for her father. She wasn't sure she was ready to talk about it just yet.

Certainly these days she had a more open mind about what was reality and what was in the realm of possibility. The idea of Skinwalkers no longer seemed like a fantasy. But that was only a minor blip in what had turned out to be life-altering changes.

Her former work for NASA didn't hold nearly the same fascination as it had before. She'd come to the conclusion that her best course of action would be to put in a request to become a contracted consultant like her father.

Working on limited and part-time projects sounded like a great idea for now. It would allow her the time to do the other things she'd decided were most important in life.

Things like volunteering to help others. She wasn't sure yet exactly where or how, but she was convinced that helping people was what she was meant to do. Since she'd managed to assist the Brotherhood with their war, she'd discovered a new way of thinking about life's true meaning.

But somewhere buried inside her gut, Reagan knew that one of her reasons for change was purely selfish. Helping others would take her mind off the pain of not seeing Kody.

Shirley Nez's smile widened. "The Dine are worthy of your consideration."

"What?" This time it was almost as if the woman had actually read her mind.

"You appear to be at a crossroads in life. We have come to ask for your help, and hope you will consider what we have to say."

"Oh? Well, yes. I'm willing to listen."

Both women nodded, while their faces grew somber. In low tones, they explained the Brotherhood's growing need for her technological and scientific expertise. She asked them several questions, mostly about living arrangements and workloads. But the big questions stayed buried in her heart.

"So, I would be living in your home, Mrs. Long? With you?" Reagan was afraid to ask where Kody would be. Neither of the women had mentioned him at all.

Kody's mother smiled. "The Begay clan has not yet been consulted, but this old woman has decided it is time for change. I will be marrying soon, and moving to Farmington."

"Marrying? Who?" Now wasn't that just the rudest question? Reagan hoped Mrs. Long would forgive her.

"Once again, I will be joining with an Anglo," Mrs. Long answered openly. "But the man I join this time has a large clan of his own. Many grown children and grandchildren."

"How wonderful for you," Reagan blurted.

Suddenly she could see that the older woman must be deeply in love. It was right there in her eyes. Reagan wondered if that same look was in her own eyes.

"I hope my sons will see the vision of my future with your eyes," Mrs. Long said wryly.

"The Brotherhood needs your help, my child," Shirley stated. "They will arrange for you to be comfortable. And I will be there to be sure they do."

The whole Brotherhood? Did that include Kody?

"But I thought the People were prejudiced against whites," she began hesitantly. "Will they make my life difficult?"

Mrs. Long touched her arm. "No one can make your life difficult but you. If you come to Dinetah with an open heart, and if your truest wish is to help and to learn the Way, then the People will be open and giving in return.

"I only hope I will find my new Anglo clan and neighbors to be so open and giving," Kody's mother added with a touch of wistfulness.

"I can't imagine anyone, anywhere, not loving you immediately." Reagan almost cried, thinking of how much she would miss talking to Mrs. Long on the phone. "I'll really miss you."

"I won't be far, daughter. An hour or two at most. We can still speak on the telephone. And I've agreed with the man who will be my new husband that I should learn what he calls 'e-mail.' You do such a thing, do you not?"

Reagan smiled, even way down in her soul, where dark loneliness had been her emotional companion for weeks now. She talked on with the two older women another few minutes, but no one seemed ready to talk about Kody.

She wasn't positive she could stand to live on the reservation, being nearby and working with him, and never… never… That just might take much more courage than she'd found over the last month. Battling Skinwalkers and saving her father had not prepared her for the most daring undertaking of her life.

Reagan found she had no choice but to ask the burning questions. She had to open the subject, even if the answers were going to hurt. There didn't seem to be any way around it.

"What does Kody have to say about all this? Will he mind working with me?"

"Kody won't mind a bit." The deep voice coming from behind her surprised her, but she would've known it anywhere. "And he has quite a lot to say about all this."

"Kody?" She swung around in her seat. Wanting with all her heart to get up and go to him, she wasn't sure her shaky legs would take her that far.

Fortunately, he walked to her side, watching her closely as he held out his hand. "Will you excuse us, my mothers?" he asked the older women without glancing over at them. "Can I have a few words with you…alone, Red?"

His face was a mask. It was impossible to tell what he was thinking or what he wanted to say. This was exactly the kind of thing she hated the most about not being able to understand other people.

If only he was just another mathematical equation…

She managed a nod and let him draw her out of her chair and outside to his uncle's patio. For winter, the day was sweltering, with insects buzzing and power lawn mowers grinding away in the distance. But Reagan barely noticed a thing save that he still had hold of her hand.

"Have you figured out what's really going on yet, love?" he asked while pulling a lawn chair around.

His eyes seemed to be brimming with an emotion she couldn't recognize. And she was suddenly reminded of just how gorgeous he really was. Of how much she loved the way his mouth quirked up at the sides whenever he looked at her that way.

Had he asked her something? "Uh…what?"

He smiled and she felt it all the way down in her toes. Falling backward into the chair, she watched as he drew another chair up beside her.

"It took me until a couple of hours ago to really *get* the idea myself." He picked up her hand and held it as though she might disappear if he didn't grasp it tightly. "I thought it had to do with loneliness."

"Huh?"

"You know," he said, and waved his free hand between them. "You…me…us. I thought we were two lonely people who'd found each other. I thought we were both misfits who needed each other because we didn't have anyone else. And I figured being alone was the reason I've been so irritable and useless without you."

She blinked a couple of times. He was irritable? Him?

He chuckled. "Yeah. Hard to believe, huh?" Rolling his eyes, he continued, "Finally I got so down and depressed that the Brotherhood had to intercede."

He quickly added, when she twisted up her mouth, "They *do* need your help. Don't imagine that was a scam just to get you back to Dinetah for my sake. But I should've seen it for myself. I should've been the one who thought to—"

"Wait a sec," she interrupted, tugging at her hand. "The Brotherhood had to *make* you decide you needed me? You suddenly recognized my worth because they interceded on my behalf? I'm not sure I want to hear that."

He actually grinned as he tightened his grip again. "Typical. I'm not getting the words right. But don't you see? That's exactly why I thought we needed to be together. You aren't the best orator in the bunch, either."

With that, she managed to jerk her hand away. Folding her arms over her chest, she glared at him.

"Damn. You are so adorable. I can't…" Kody stood and pulled her to her feet.

Gathering her in his arms, he kissed her. Kissed her as though he might not survive another minute if he didn't.

His familiar masculine scent brought her home. Back safely to the refuge she had so missed.

She almost believed. And almost cried because she so badly wanted to believe.

Kody drew his head back just far enough to gaze into her eyes. But he didn't release her, even though she squirmed and tried to escape his embrace.

Everything was too sharp for her to stand it. And too edgy. Teetering on a precipice of potential agony.

"It isn't a question of what the Brotherhood needs," he said while brushing aside a curl from her cheek. "Or even of saving the Dine. And it's especially not about two lonely people needing each other."

Holding her breath, she wondered if she could bear hearing what he had to say. It was too intense.

"I finally realized it's not just about sharing another person's burdens, but about letting them take some of your own burdens. I was willing to help *you* with coming face-to-face with your father and with fighting the Skinwalkers, but I wasn't ready to share any of *my* problems with you in return.

"Now I am, Red," he said with a wide smile. "I've gotten it through my thick skull that life's problems grow easier when they're shared. You didn't face the snake Skinwalker all by yourself, and neither did I. We beat him together. That's what family and clans do for each other.

"Will you come back and help me face the rest of our life's burdens?" he finally asked.

"Why?"

His laugh this time was full of delight and joy. "Trust a genius to break it down to the lowest denominator. Good question.

"And the answer is, Reagan Wilson, because I love you."

His eyes were luminescent and grew damp as he waited for her to say something. But her own tears were on the verge of choking the words right out of her throat.

He leaned in and kissed her forehead. "Come home with me, my darling genius. Our home. Together we'll make our own place in the world and keep it safe from evil.

"Make a family with me," he added with a sigh. "Because you love me, too, and want to share your life."

The tears streamed down her face. Tears of happiness. Tears that would become a loving trail, taking them straight to their future.

"Yes," she managed to answer through her tears.

The *blessed* tears of finally knowing right where she belonged.

Epilogue

Off in an isolated corner of Dinetah, a well-dressed man eased back from his bank of computers. The sheik's money had been safely transferred and would be invested in brand-new technology, used to bring more Navajo converts to the dark side.

Rubbing his hands together, the Navajo Wolf tried to keep his body temperature close to the normal level. A tiny niggle of worry about the many changes going on in his human form sneaked into his mind. But he pushed it back out.

The ancient ones would not have left the secret parchments with instructions for overtaking the world by using Skinwalker methods had there been any danger of being killed by following their guidelines. All the Wolf needed now was to translate a few more pages. Pages he was sure must contain further secrets for staying healthy while continuing to change over to the evil side on a daily basis.

He never gave a single thought to the Brotherhood. Or to the half-breed and the Anglo woman who were about to join forces to find and capture him.

The Snake had lost the last battle. But the Wolf would win the war.

Darkness had begun creeping over the world in the form of terrorism and mass destruction. But the Wolf delighted in the fact that it was only a beginning to the skirmishes that must be fought in the final war between evil and good.

Such had been ordained by the ancient ones. And the Navajo Wolf was the one who would make it happen.

* * * * *

Don't miss the next book in Linda Conrad's
wonderful new NIGHT GUARDIANS *series,*
SHADOW WATCH,
available May 2006
wherever Silhouette Books are sold.

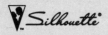

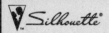

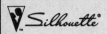

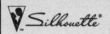